Rising Up
on
Ordinary Days

Rising Up on Ordinary Days

Judy McGinn

Rising Up on Ordinary Days© 2023 Judy McGinn

ISBN 978-1-957221-11-3

All Rights Reserved. Permission to reprint individual poems must be obtained from the author who owns the copyright.

Printed in the United States of America
FIRST EDITION

Clare Songbirds Publishing House
140 Cottage Street
Auburn, New York 13021
www.claresongbirdspub.com

This book is dedicated to my sons, Brendan McGinn and Seamus McGinn, and to my late husband, Michael, who always believed I could do anything I set my mind to.

Acknowledgements

Grateful acknowledgement is given to the editors and publishers of the following publications where these short stories first appeared.

"A Sea Change" was first published in *Synkroniciti*, November, 2021. "Lilies of the Field" won first prize in prose in *Cork Literary Review, Poetry, Prose & Drama*, Vol.II. "Secret Burial" first appeared in *The South Carolina Review*, Volume 37, Fall. "Losing Zan Gambol" first appeared in *The South Carolina Review*, Volume 34, Spring.

I would like to thank my sister, Barbara (Brooke) Mobley, for being first reader of many of these stories, and for her unending encouragement to keep going. Thanks to Maureen McCarthy who read this collection and supported me in countless ways. My thanks to the Pen Women Writers Group, and friends: Mary Gardner, Nancy Dafoe, Karen Hempson, Bobbie Panek and Janine DeBaise for their edits and much laughter. My gratitude to Heidi Nightengale and Laura Williams French the publishers at Clare Songbirds Publishing House for believing in me, and my friend Rachael Ikins, for helping me on this journey.

Contents

A Sea Change
1

Secret Burial
13

Losing Zan Gambol
31

Good Intentions
49

Caught in the Undertow
65

Sticks and Stones
75

Lilies in the Field
87

Throne of the Third Heaven
95

Piano Lessons
109

Dreams in Deep Water
115

A Sea Change

Jane stood on tiptoe and stretched to place a willow-pattern platter in the top of a kitchen cupboard when pain assaulted her. It slammed into the left side of her face, from the top of her teeth, across the sinus cavity and bone beneath her eye. The dish slipped from her hand, shattered, and bounced up and out on the tile in a frenzied blue fountain. She slid from the counter, down the drawers in slow motion like a raw egg and puddled on the floor.

Claire, her 19-year-old daughter, barreled in. "Mom! What happened?" She squatted to look her mother in the eye. Jane shook her head, laid it onto tented knees and groaned.

"Mom! What's wrong? What should I do? You're scaring me!"

Jane lifted watery eyes and mouthed "Dad", then shoved a fist into her mouth to muffle a moan. Claire flew in search of her father.

A panting David soon appeared. "Are you all right?" He knelt beside Jane and squeezed her hand. "Claire said you fell. What hurts?"

Jane twisted her head sideways and stared at him. "The strangest thing…" the sentence flitted away like a butterfly. Her gaze skittered past the sink, hovered at the open window with a view of the leafy maple David had planted when Spencer, their youngest, was born. She dragged her eyes onto Claire, "I'm feeling a little stunned, almost like I was punched in the face. Sorry I scared you, honey."

David helped her up. "Are you sure you're okay?"

She nodded, wiped her clothes, and asked Claire to grab a broom and dustpan.

"I thought you were having a stroke or something," Claire said.

"I'm okay. Maybe it's a tooth abscess. I think I'll call Dr. Burk and see if she can fit me in." She tentatively touched her cheek and went to fill the kettle for a cup of tea. "I'm fine, David, although I'm not sure what happened." David shook his head and headed out of the kitchen.

After sweeping up the broken china, Claire slipped away.

Moments later, the aroma and taste of Barry's Gold Blend brought Jane to a more comfortable state, the pain now reduced to a dull throb. She ripped a page from the TO DO list on the fridge and scribbled between sips.

Her cell phone plinked a xylophone one-liner. It was Jerry Barrett, the Calvert High School baseball coach. He said that Spencer had been hit with a baseball and was on his way to the Emergency Care Center in Prince Frederick for an x-ray; could she meet him there?

Jane's pulse quickened. "Spencer is injured?"

Coach Barrett's nasal-heavy drawl clapped against her ear. "He seems fine, up walking around. It's just a precaution."

"Where was he hit?"

"I'm afraid it was smack in the face from a power drive to the infield. Even if nothing is broken, he's going to have one heck of a shiner."

"How awful! When did it happen?"

"About ten minutes ago. Bobby, you know my assistant coach, took him right away. Like I say, there's no reason to panic. I think he's fine." Jane shivered involuntarily and refused to acknowledge the idea that surfaced. She grabbed her purse and hurried to the car.

Spence, at eighteen, had managed to survive a crammed sports schedule without major injury throughout high school. In the years before he got his license, Jane had lived under the tyranny of his schedule, since she drove him almost everywhere. She had relished the thought of his sixteenth birthday when getting his driver's license promised her the luxury of freedom, but she hadn't envisioned how, in reality, that diminished their time together. Conversations with him about everyday issues instantly ceased. Now, he was just weeks away from starting his freshman year at Duke with the aim of a degree in marine biology.

Weekends at the Riley's were busy with the kids coming and going. Claire, home after completing her freshman year at Towson University, created a vortex of energy in the house surrounded by her clutch of friends. Jane was grateful for the activity, which provided a respite from the listlessness that sometimes seeped into her. It was happening with increasing frequency lately and unbidden tears sprang at random moments.

One Saturday afternoon, she headed to the basement to retrieve a piece of luggage for Spencer, to encourage him to begin packing. Stepping over bags and assorted, labeled boxes she tugged the case from a shelf and dislodged a familiar, long-forgotten object. Smiling, she rubbed her hand across the top of a dusty, wooden art box. Her fingers traced the clasp, and the box gasped open. Brushes, each one carefully considered and purchased long ago, nestled in a compartment. The smooth handles and sable bristles beckoned like old friends. She hadn't painted since grad school when an MFA had been within reach, but an unintended pregnancy intervened. A rolled, creamy canvas beckoned. Dried tubes of paint can easily be replaced, she thought, closing the lid. She carried the box and luggage upstairs.

The following week, Jane was stooped in the neglected rose bushes along the front of the house, happily pruning and clearing, when Spence backed out of the garage on his way to visit a friend. She waved and watched him drive away. Burnt blooms gone to seed needed attention. After completing the nearby bushes, she reached to pull a stray dandelion when her body felt a powerful thrust from face to chest. Momentarily stunned, she found herself sprawled out on the lawn. It took a minute or more before she struggled to sit up. The intense evening heat, combined with the strange sensation in her body, made her dizzy. She shuddered her head and chastised herself for not waiting to garden until morning when it was cooler. Rolling onto her knees, she managed to stand and slowly headed inside the house. A few gulps of ice water and the odd sensation faded to a numbing tingle on her skin.

Within five minutes Spence called. "Mom, I've been in an accident. I'm all right, but the airbag deployed."

Jane's hand flew to her chest in an unconscious effort to calm her runaway heartbeat. "Did you call the police? If not, you need to call them."

"A man who was stopped behind me at the intersection came up to see if I was okay and just called them." Spencer relayed his location to Jane and within minutes she was on her way to the scene.

The accident had caved in the passenger door and Spence was lucky. The airbag saved him from serious injury. That evening, he was released from the hospital into Jane's care with only bruises and minor abrasions caused by his catapulted cell phone. Jane tenderly tucked him in bed, grateful he was home safe. Remembering the simultaneous sensation in the garden made her uneasy, but she scolded herself she was being ridiculous. Was she losing her grip on reality?

On the 4th of July, the Rileys hosted a barbecue for David's sister, Sonia, husband Malcolm, and their three teens, who Jane felt she hardly knew anymore. They barely said hello, and spent visits bowing to their phones, as did Spence and Claire. They belonged to the Electronic Army of Teenagers, or EAT, a phrase Jane had coined out of frustration when she couldn't get them to lift their heads and look at her. Eating was the only other thing she could verify that they did.

Heat trickled into the house like molasses every time someone went in or out, despite the fully-cranked air conditioner. On the back patio, Jane and Sonia sipped frosty, lime-infused gin and tonics under the umbrella and caught up on family news while the men huddled over the grill, debating the best method to send smoke signals to the neighbors.

Spence was off with a pack of friends to Ocean City for the long weekend.

Sonia said, "Here's to remembering how sweet the kids were before puberty!" They clinked glasses, though Jane squelched a twinge of sadness that threatened to overwhelm her. She sipped her drink and idly wondered if a binky had had similar effects on her children as the alcohol offered her now.

As darkness gathered, fathers and children up and down the road retrieved fireworks purchased on trips to Pennsylvania or Georgia during the preceding twelve months and a fierce competition ensued. Halfway through the pyrotechnic display, Jane stretched out on a lawn chair and smiled blissfully.

Moments later, she clutched her throat, unable to breathe. Scrambling to her feet, she stumbled across the patio to the sliding door, knocking over an aluminum webbed chair on the way, and tore through the open door. David was inside getting a beer. Rasping noises burbled up from her throat before she dissolved onto the floor.

In two strides David reached her and dropped to his knees. He prepared for mouth-to-mouth resuscitation when Jane shoved him away. She sputtered and coughed like a car with a dying battery, and managed a gulp of air, then lay back, her chest rising and falling. David sat back on his knees. "What the hell happened?"

She shook her head from side to side on the floor. The tile felt deliciously cool against her cheeks, so she kept rolling her head back and forth. "I—couldn't—breathe."

"That's obvious, darling. I'm asking why you couldn't breathe." His eyes narrowed as her head continue to oscillate. "What are you doing that for?"

"What?"

"That thing with your head."

"Can't talk." She didn't want to tell him how soothing the tiles felt, how wonderful it was to feel anything after an encounter with her mortality.

"Well stop it! You need to sit up so we can see if you're okay. I'm becoming concerned about these bizarre episodes. They're so"—he searched for the proper word, "—dramatic."

He lifted her right arm to help her up. Fear scrambled up her spine when she stood. "Give me the phone. Hurry!" David fished in his pocket and handed it to her. She scrolled through his favorites to Spence and pushed call. A male voice answered, "Hello?"

"This is Spencer's mom. I need to talk to him."

"Just a minute." A shout sprang through the phone, "Hey, it's Spencer's mom." The phone was then covered, as Jane couldn't hear. Next, "I'm sorry, but he can't come to the phone."

Jane's pulse thrummed in her ears. "Get him *right now*!" Again, the sound was muffled.

David grabbed for the phone, but she jerked it away. Voices on the other end shouted something inaudible, then came a static sound of crashing surf. Another minute passed. A breathless male voice, "Mrs. Riley, this is Matt. Spence and a couple of guys were wrestling on the beach and he got the breath knocked out of him. He's okay now."

"I'd still like to talk to him."

Moments passed. "Hi, Mom." Spencer sounded as if he'd been running. Beyond that, he was cheerful, as if nothing had happened.

"Spence, are you all right?"

"Yes. I can't remember the last time that happened but I'm fine. What's going on there? Did Dad and Uncle Malcolm beat the pants off the neighbors in the fireworks battle?"

"It's not over yet. They're gearing up for the finale." She had to come up with a quick excuse for calling. "I just wanted to wish you happy 4th, and to remind you, if any of you have fireworks, be safe. That's an order. I'll let you get back to your friends."

She pressed end, laid her head on her arms at the kitchen counter, and breathed a sigh of relief. When she raised her eyes, she found David staring at her in a way the judges on *America's Got Talent* might stare at a contortionist. "What?" she asked.

"You know what. I want to understand what just happened."

Jane looked at her husband of twenty years, took a deep breath and explained how she had just experienced Spencer's pain.

"Are you drunk?"

"Don't be insulting."

"How did you know that's what it was?"

She explained the other two instances.

There was a long pause before David said gently, "You've been stressed out lately. Maybe you should see someone—a therapist."

"Thank you for your support. How do you think that conversation might go? The shrink says tell me, Mrs. Riley, what seems to be the problem? I say I feel my child's pain. He says, ma'am, we're parents; we all do. Then I say, no, you don't understand. I feel his physical pain, and proceed to tell him what I just told you, and he scribbles notes about the delusional woman in his office while he thinks about where to commit me. It's not in my head, David. It's real. You just witnessed it. They've documented that twins can experience each other's pain. Why not a mother and child? But the shrink is going to say it's impossible, that I'm crazy, and pretty soon guys in white coats are going to show up to take me away. Let's keep this secret between us, all right? Aside from this weird phenomenon, I don't perceive any other psychological problems. Do you? Although they do say a mentally ill person is the last to know."

"Not that I've noticed. But maybe I haven't been as attentive as I should have been lately."

"B.S. David! Ooooooh, I have psychic powers. Or whatever this is that's been happening." She plucked a glass from the cupboard, filled it with ice water, and followed him outside. Soon staccato explosions of red and blue bloomed like a chrysanthemum garden in the sky. Jane and Sonia clapped rapidly, shouted, "Bravo! Bravo!"

July melted into August and Spence's circled departure date loomed. David, Jane, Spence and his friend, Conor, were to spend the last weekend together on the boat. They planned to go to Solomon's Island and moor overnight. The day before Jane had removed the canvas from the art box, attached it to new stretcher bars and packed them both in the car along with new paint tubes and an easel. After a mega shop at Super Giant, she stuffed the cooler with essentials: a bouquet of chicken necks as crab bait, beer, and sodas to keep the guys docile, a bottle of her favorite sauvignon blanc, along with groceries.

The four of them boarded *Cat's Pajamas* and David eased the boat from the slip at the marina. The Chesapeake Bay opened wide before them and they turned southward. The boys dangled their legs off the bow, laughing as the spray splashed them. Jane watched from the galley while she secured groceries in cubicles. A wistful smile tugged at her lips and she felt an ache of time fleeting seeing Spence acting like a carefree kid. She fished Coppertone from the miscellaneous drawer and went on deck. Once the sunscreen was slathered on, she plopped on an Orioles cap and reclined in a deck chair to watch the passing landscape.

Sometime later David pointed the bow inland and Flag Pond Park slipped into view. Jane looked at the deserted ribbon of sand protected beyond by cattails and water grasses. An osprey lifted into the air as the boat glided in. David shouted for Spence to throw out the anchor and he cut the engine. The quiet was heightened after the rush of wind and clamor of boats in the center of the bay.

"Dad, this place is awesome!" Spence said as he unraveled

the anchor rope. He chased Conor to push him overboard. Conor squealed a karate-type yell and jumped in. Spence followed with a running cannonball.

For the first time in months, a sense of peace washed over Jane followed by an irresistible urge to paint. It was like greeting a close friend who had moved far away, and you have years to catch up on. She set up the easel and squeezed spirals of paint onto a board, lost in paradise. Time was suspended until the midday sun pulled her back to reality and the sparkling water beckoned. Art supplies were quickly stowed, and she informed David she was going for a swim.

Diving in, she soon found a rhythm in an easy freestyle stroke, the lift and stretch and glide through the water. Her mind cleared of everything but her body movement in the current, cutting through a wave, riding a swell. She was so engrossed in the freedom that when looking up for a location check, she was alarmed to see the boat in the distance almost a hundred yards away. As a small object floating in the water, she was vulnerable to boats cruising by. She began turning when too late a swirling clot of jellyfish lurking beneath the surface caught her attention. A spidery film enclosed her legs and right arm. She thrashed and kicked until they slithered off.

Pain burned like a torch on her skin. She stared longingly at the boat and panic shot through her, threatened to pull her under. Instead of reverting to a long stroke she frantically started to dog paddle, thwarting her effort to swim against the current. Survival instinct flared at last and she resumed freestyle. All her energy focused on extending each stroke. When at last her fingertips brushed the ladder, she pulled herself up and flopped onto the deck like a limp clump of seaweed. "Help!" she squeaked. She imagined *The Baltimore Sun* headline "Death by Jellyfish." I wonder how the family would react. Would they be more grief-stricken or more embarrassed?

David materialized above her. "Did something happen to you or is this another one of those I-feel-Spence's-pain episodes?"

She moved her lips like a guppy, then sat up in alarm. "Where's Spence?"

"He's fine. The boys are crabbing off the bow."

Relieved, she pointed to her legs. Seeing the purple swathe swelling on Jane's extremities, David helped her to the nearest seat. "I'll be right back." He returned with a bottle of vinegar and cotton balls and began bathing where she was stung.

The remedy cooled the burning and she said, "Look on the bright side. This is the first time in a while it's been *my* pain."

"Hallelujah!" David said.

Under his gentle ministrations, the pain became bearable. "Could I have a nice salad and a little olive oil to go with this, please?"

Afterward, she watched as David pulled one of the crab traps up hand-over-hand. Nine blue-green crabs scrabbled for the chicken necks. Dumping the others into a bushel basket, he let the trap down again. The second trap held seven, not counting two Sallies, and a soft-shell male, which he tossed back.

"At this rate, we'll have plenty for a feast," Jane said. "I'll check the starboard line before we head to Solomon's." She slowly reeled in the line, feeling the weight of it. It held five good-size crabs, their blue-tipped claws grappling for the raw chicken.

Light spread across the water with the waning sun and they pulled anchor and motored toward Solomon's Island. Once tied at the dock of the marina the boys bowed their heads to their cell phones. Jane turned on the CD player and hummed along to Norah Jones' old hit "Come Away with Me", while she shucked corn. David placed the crabs in a large pot of boiling water and soon the aroma of Old Bay Seasoning magically pulled the boys toward food and they helped set the table. The four of them gleefully pounded the crabs with mallets. Spence declared the feast was crabulous, and afterward, Jane said she would clean up and released the boys, who leaped onto the dock and headed to the village.

David and Jane stretched out under the sky and sipped the remainder of their drinks. The stars were brilliant. The moment stirred their passion, offering an illusion of being young again, if only for a few minutes.

Later, Jane read the next chapter of Anne Tyler's *The Beginner's Goodbye* and waited for the boys' return. Just past eleven, they scrambled below to the aft cabin. Jane couldn't sleep. After tossing about for half an hour, she slid out of bed and went on deck to feel again the soft summer night.

On the shore lights flared in windows like a runaway fire. Laughter and the occasional phrase flew past like night birds. She thought about when the kids were small before they lived near the bay. Tears trickled down her cheeks. They used to go camping every summer. When Spence was five, they camped on Assateague Island, and one night a herd of wild ponies came snuffling through the campsite. Spence clambered onto her lap and clung to her, his eyes wide with fear. Peach-colored moonlight spilled across the ocean. Silhouetted against the sky, a dark pony came within feet of their open tent. It lowered its head to where they were sitting and looked straight at them. They stared back at the fringed, dark globes, the velvet muzzle with nostrils flaring in and out, puffing little clouds of earthy breath. Spence quivered with excitement and wrinkled his nose against the wild smell. At the sound of a distant whinny, the pony reeled and galloped over the dunes. The next morning, hoof prints in the sand were the only evidence they had ever been there at all.

Secret Burial

When the devil came to possess my family, the summer I was nine, I knew it was my fault. It started with the fact that my daddy was big on memorizing Bible verses. He was dedicated to offering his children to the service of the Lord and he'd make sure we were worthy even if it meant spending our entire childhood sitting in a corner with a Bible. He didn't believe in sparing the rod either. Many's the time I bore punishment of a switch on bare legs for some sin. That was never the end of it for Daddy, though. After what he called corporal punishment, he banished me to the glider on the front porch to pore over a passage in the New Testament, usually Matthew, and learned it off by heart. Locked in misery, I watched the disappearing backs of my younger brother and sister running off to play, watched freedom leaving me, kicked up in little clouds of sand from their bare feet like bursts of tiny stars. It got to where I hated the disciples for writing their doggone books, especially Matthew, since he seemed to be Daddy's favorite. I reckon God and the Devil both knew how I felt and that was why the Devil chose to move in with us that summer.

The one advantage of memorizing verses was that in Sunday school, for knowing certain Bible passages you earned a badge that was presented during preaching. Daddy brought back the badges from the National Conference of Independent Bible Churches in Raleigh early that spring. I was in the throes of my tomboy stage and was determined to get the sword badge for memorizing a passage of Romans. By June I was ready to impress him with my recitation.

On Sunday morning, I leaped from the porch over three steps and landed on my knees in the sand, barely shook myself off before galloping to the car. It had been two days since I'd been released from the prison of Mrs. Friscoe's third-grade class and I felt free as the butterflies flitting around the sunflowers stretching up the side of the house. It had been a difficult year from the start, as I saw no useful purpose in learning multiplication tables. I decided shortly after school started that my future lay in any direction that led me away from arithmetic. Mrs. Friscoe did not share my view and we had problems all year with me getting sent to the principal's office more than once due to what she called my "stubborn streak." Daddy claimed it came from Mama's side, but she said it definitely came down through the Miller line, along with red hair, a tendency toward fanaticism, and a hair-trigger temper.

While we rattled past tobacco fields to Pleasant Hill Bible Church where Daddy was preacher, I closed my eyes and inhaled Mama's gardenia perfume and imagined myself on a tropical island surrounded by palm trees and waiters who brought me sweet scuppernong grapes when I snapped my fingers.

Daddy's voice brought me back to the stuffy station wagon where I was packed between Gene and Parker, two of my brothers. "Who's first to recite your Bible verses today?"

"Please, can I go first?" I said, before anyone else could volunteer. "Romans 3:13-26. 'Their throat is an open sepulcher; with their tongues they have used deceit, the poison of asps is under their lips…'"

"Romans, that's a good one. That's fine," said Daddy. That was high praise from him, and I grinned with pride. Mama looked at us in the back seat. "Who'd like to go next? Gene, how about you? Did you learn off any this week?"

Gene shook his head, shrugged and closed his eyes. Parker blurted out, "Jesus wept,'" and hooted while slapping his knee. He did the same thing every Sunday.

"That's good, dear," said Mama, pretending it was the first time she'd heard it. She patted Daddy on the shoulder when he turned toward her and clenched the muscles in his jaw.

After Sunday school Sister Parker, my teacher, filled in a card and sent it to Daddy so I could get the longed-for badge. I hurried to the front pew reserved for our family.

"Stop fidgeting," Mama whispered in my ear as my legs made sucking noises when I lifted one and then the other off the pew. It was so hot even the paper fan from Brock's Funeral Home that Mama swished at me didn't cool me down. After the doxology Daddy presented the badges.

"This week it is my pleasure to call my daughter, April, to stand with me and receive an award for memorizing Romans, chapter 3, verses 13 to 26."

I stepped forward and blushed, another trait that plagued me like sin. He took the sword-shaped badge covered in shiny silver paper and pinned it on my collar. From the handle curled three colored satin ribbons. He said each one symbolized a different aspect of Christ's life: white for purity, red for death, and purple for resurrection.

I could hardly sit still through the rest of the service. I fingered the ribbons dangling from the badge as I stole glances at the sword. I thought of gallant knights bravely defending ladies in long sweeping gowns on winding staircases of castles far away from the plain, white walls of the church, the polished heart-of-pine cross behind the altar. The sun poured through the open windows on our side making the room so hot it started to smell like sweaty grownups, so I tried to concentrate on Mama's fading gardenia.

I was drifting into a daydream when Daddy pounded the pulpit and I jumped two inches off the pew. He grabbed hold of the pulpit with both hands, leaned forward and roared. He was scary when he started shouting about sin.

It was like when he yelled at Parker for cussing or fighting. He'd get so mad he'd start shaking. First thing you know, he'd yank off his belt and light into him. After one awful beating earlier that summer, I sat on Parker's lap, patting him on the back while he cried into my shoulder. I was crying too and at that minute I hated Daddy. I wished I could cut a big fat switch to use on him so he'd know what it felt like to be beat like that.

After supper that night I went looking for him. He was on the front porch glider staring at the stars. "Hey there," he said. "Look up yonder. There's the big dipper." He pointed to the constellation so brilliant in the black sky.

I refused to be distracted. "Daddy, how can you be so hateful to Parker? He can't help the way he is." My lip started to quiver but I stood my ground, arms crossed. He looked at me for a long time without speaking. In a faraway voice he said, "I'm going to tell you something I haven't told anybody but your mother. Sit down here." He patted the seat beside him and I obeyed. He put his arm around me and drew me close. Parker has a character weakness, so the devil takes hold of him. God is putting my faith through fire when the devil makes your brother do what he does. God told me I had to beat it out of him; it's the only way. It kills me to have to do it, Sugar. It's like Abraham being willing to kill his son Isaac, if that was what God wanted him to do. Believe me, it's harder on me than it is on him."

I instantly doubted that, since I had felt the pain of a switch myself, but I trembled to think the devil could get inside my brother and dreaded turning the light off that night. For once I was glad Faye and I shared a room.

Daddy also said God gave him the texts of his sermons and that morning, while I squirmed in the heat, I wondered if God had given him a long or a short one this time. He preached about the rapture. He said born-again Christians would be taken to heaven, plucked off the face of the earth, out of fields, houses, schools, beauty parlors. I wondered if they'd disappear from behind steering wheels of cars and trucks and imagined thousands of wrecks all around the world. Then I got to thinking about Parker and how the Devil got in him and wondered what would happen to him if the rapture came during what Daddy called a possession, if he would be left behind. One thought led to another and I figured if the Devil could get inside Parker, then he could get in me, maybe even in the whole family, except Daddy, of course, since he was on visiting terms with God.

His voice dropped to a whisper, a signal he was near the end. Nobody went forward during the invitational hymn, but I felt a nudge inside me. Off and on all day his sermon kept popping into my head, that and the idea the Devil might get me.

I was saved that night at the evening service. The altar call hymn was "Just As I Am," which always made me emotional. In gentle tones Daddy gave the invitation. "Jesus is waiting for you. Won't you come?"

An irresistible inner force propelled me to the front of the church. Mama came and knelt beside me, though it was awkward in her condition. Together we prayed for Jesus to come into my heart. I felt so new, so clean. To me it was God speaking and not my daddy when he spoke about angels rejoicing in heaven and quoted Jesus, "Suffer the little children to come unto me." He came over to where Mama and I were praying and knelt on the other side of me. When I finally stood, he helped Mama struggle up, then hugged me so tight and so long it made me cry. My feelings were all jumbled up between getting saved and having both my parents all to myself for once and them being so happy. I wondered if I would ever feel that special again in my whole life and tried to make the moment last.

The following Sunday I was baptized in the Seneca River wearing a dreamy blue dress Mama bought me at Belk's department store for the ceremony. When we walked into the girls' department at Belk's the dress was on a mannequin and Mama had sighed. "Oh!" I knew instantly what she would say next. It was one of her stories from her own childhood, how her daddy had some kind of windfall and brought home three dresses one day. It was the only time in her life he had bought her anything not connected with chores or school. To have one store-bought dress was bliss, but three! My mother thought she must be imagining things. One of them was a sailor dress and she had jumped up and down with joy over it; something she never dared dream might be hers, and now it was under their roof, spread out in royal blue beauty on the couch. On impulse her daddy had invited a neighbor girl, who had been visiting my mama, to come in and suddenly, in what my mother was convinced to this day was an innate desire to hurt her, offered her friend first choice of the three, and of course, she chose the sailor dress. Mama had been crushed with disappointment and never got over it. Here was a sailor dress, and I knew her buying it for me was tangled up in that earlier experience of her childhood. Now I knew what she meant. How I loved that dress with its snowy collar and scarlet tie. It had one deep pocket trimmed in white piping. I thought it was the most beautiful dress I had ever seen.

The morning of my baptism Mama put my hair in two pigtails, pinned the sword badge to my collar, and said, "You've made me so happy," as she wrapped her gardenia smell around me.

The congregation walked from the church through the woods to the riverbank. Sister Parker came up and held onto me while I balanced on one foot and removed my shoes and socks. "Whoa there," she said, unpinned the badge and placed it into a shoe. Before I could make a getaway, Lucy skipped up to us. "Hey, April." She twisted to and fro in what I thought was a new dress of purple gingham checks with a white sash. I didn't comment on it, which I hoped aggravated her. Ever since the time I had stayed overnight at Sister Parker's house I had resented Lucy. She lived two houses down from Sister Parker. I used to like her and thought she was nice, but it turned out my judgment was incorrect.

The humiliation of that day still stung every time I thought about it. We had been playing "Mother-May-I." She was sitting on the top step of her porch and I was halfway down the sidewalk. I called out for her to jump off the steps onto the side of the house and she forgot to say Mother may I. When I reminded her, she got all weird like I'd done something wrong and then turned around and pushed a big clay pot of red geraniums on the top step crashing to the sidewalk. Dirt and flower petals went everywhere, the clay pot in crooked shards spreading out onto the grass. Her mother came out and demanded to know what happened and Lucy blamed me, said I had knocked it over jumping off the porch. I tried to explain my side to her mother but she stuck by her own and told me it was time I went back home. In utter embarrassment, I ran back to Sister Parker's crying, my face feeling like it was on fire. For the longest time I refused to tell her what had happened because I was so humiliated. It was one thing for my brother or sister to blame me for something they did, but that was to my own parents. I'd never be able to face Lucy's mother again. Sister Parker was so upset she threatened to go talk to Lucy's mom to find out what was wrong, so I told her. After I finished crying, I said, "It's so unfair!" She sat at the kitchen table shelling peas, thinking to herself and finally said, "You never know why other people act the way they do until you've walked around in their shoes. Maybe she would have gotten a terrible spanking and knew her mother wouldn't do anything to you; so, don't be too hard on her. We shouldn't judge people when we don't have all the facts." I didn't say anything, but I thought about it and figured I *had* all the facts and from that day on I thought of (and referred to) that girl as Lying Lucy.

At my baptism I barely said hello as I pushed past her. "Daddy's waiting for me," I said, and waded into the river, the shifting, sandy bed scratching between my toes. When the water was up to my chest we stopped and faced the shore. Daddy said a few words about Jesus' baptism by John and gave me the prearranged signal to hold my nose. He placed his hand over mine. "I baptize you in the name of the Father," he thrust me under the rushing current, "and the Son," he pushed me under again; "and the Holy Spirit." The third and final time I came up spluttering. I fought my way to shore, my dress clinging to me like wet fur, while the choir sang "Shall We Gather at the River" mingled with shouts of "Hallelujah!" and "Amen!"

That week Mama started having trouble with the baby and because she was so far along, the doctor ordered her to take it easy. Daddy hired Sister Loraine from church to help with the housework. The next evening while I was in the tobacco barn during a game of hide and seek, Faye, who was It, screamed, "April, come quick! Mama's sick!" I raced to the house to find Mama ghostly pale and so weak she couldn't walk. Daddy wrapped her in a quilt, even though it was sweltering, and carried her to the car.

He said to Gene, "You're in charge. I'll stop and get Loraine on my way home." Seeing our worried faces he added, "Don't y'all worry now. Your Mama's going to be fine. She just needs some rest. I'll be home as soon as I can."

"Parker, you do what Gene says now, y'hear?" He glared at Parker till he got a promise. As he drove away, we were left hanging silently on the front porch like a sack of kittens abandoned by the side of the road.

A few days later I was awakened by the sound of giggling from my parents' room next door. I had often heard Daddy's throaty laugh sliding over Mama's silky one. A faint alarm went off in my mind. Mama was still in the hospital.

I threw back the covers and slid my feet to the floor. When I reached the door, I tapped lightly and went to enter the room. To my surprise, it was locked. I knocked again. "Daddy, what're you doin'?" I called softly, trying not to wake the others.

"Nothin', Sugar. I'm just getting' up. You go on back to bed now, y'hear?" Something about the sound of his voice drew me down to the keyhole. Like a moth pulled into the back draft of a fan, I had to look.

The room was lit by slits of sun through slanted blinds. I slapped my hand over my mouth to keep from screaming. Loraine was lying in bed beside Daddy! The sheet was around her waist, and she was naked from there up. She had melon-shaped boobies poking towards the ceiling. A rushing sound flooded my ears like when they filled up under the downspout during a summer rainstorm. My mouth felt parched. Part of me wanted to run as fast and as far as I could, but I was locked there. I stayed. I watched. I saw Daddy rub her in slow, smooth circles for a very long time. His hand slid down her stomach and plunged under the sheet. My cheeks flushed and I clutched the doorknob to keep from falling. A tickly, queasy feeling clawed at my stomach. For a minute I thought I was going to fall down.

Loraine pulled my father's hand out and said, "For goodness' sake, Preacher, your daughter's awake in the next room; have you no shame?" He moaned and covered his head with the sheet. She giggled again as she leaped up revealing her curved, naked body. As she slipped on her robe, she blew Daddy a kiss and disappeared through the other door.

I crawled along the wooden floor back to my bed and dragged myself into it. I lay there, eyes closed, trying to forget what I had witnessed. For a time, it was quiet and I began to think maybe it had been a dream; it hadn't really happened. After while I heard sounds in the kitchen. I recognized the clatter of dishes, the oven door opening and closing. The smell of sizzling ham and hot biscuits drifted through the house and pulled me in to breakfast.

All through the meal Daddy pretended nothing had happened. He chatted with Gene about the day's work like always, although he seemed unusually cheerful. "Loraine, pass me another biscuit. I reckon they're about the best biscuits in Cumberland County."

"You always say Mama's biscuits are the best in the county," said Gene, pointing out something we all knew but Loraine.

"They're both blue ribbon winners," he said. I was relieved Daddy let the comment pass without argument. I decided to wait and see what explanation he would offer about he and Loraine. I waited all day and the next and the next.

Folks from church dropped by with casseroles and pies. One morning while Loraine was outside, Sisters Parker and Robeson knocked on the front door. "Hey there, April. We brought y'all a few things."

I opened the door and they stepped in and followed me into the kitchen. Sister Robeson, the older of the two, placed a casserole dish on the table and my mouth watered at the sight of her famous chicken and dumplings.

I made a pecan pie just for you," Sister Parker said, smiling sweetly. I blushed and looked down at my dirty bare feet. "You did say that's your favorite, didn't you?"

"Yes, ma'am. Thank you." I couldn't keep from grinning that she had remembered and baked it just for me.

"How are you children getting on without your mama?"

"Just fine, ma'am. I miss her something awful though."

"Do you know when she'll be allowed home?"

"Daddy said she might can come home this week."

Sister Robeson ran a finger along the stove top and inspected it. "By the way, where is Sister Loraine?"

"In the garden picking beans for supper."

The women instantly headed for the bedrooms, poking in closets, checking the bathroom cabinet, with me on their heels. Feeling slightly uncomfortable about this intrusion I followed them from room to room. "What are y'all looking for? Can I help?"

Sister Robeson dripped a smile on me. "Just checking to make sure Sister Loraine is doing her job while your mama's gone."

After a few minutes of me trailing after them, they said good-bye and left.

Mama was released from the hospital after ten days but was ordered to stay in bed until the baby came. I was thrilled to have her home and delighted in bringing her frosty glasses of iced tea. Sometimes I sat on the edge of her bed while she read poems by Elizabeth Barrett Browning or Emily Dickinson or sections of *A Southern Lady's Complete Guide to Etiquette*. Those were happy times when I forgot my confusion over what I had seen.

A few evenings after she returned home two grim-faced deacons arrived to see Daddy. Faye and I were sent from the room. Later, as I lay cocooned in darkness, I could hear voices raised in anger, though words were muffled. I listened and wondered.

The next morning Loraine was gone and Daisy, a woman from across the back field, was in the kitchen cooking.

"Good morning."

"Good morning. Where's Loraine?"

"I don't know her, honey. Preacher come to my house last night and said he needed my help, and asked if I could come this morning. I told him of course I'd come. Would you like some grits with red-eye gravy and scrambled eggs?"

"Yes, ma'am. Thank you." I tried to find out from Gene what had happened but he maintained a tight-lipped silence.

When Sunday came, I presented myself to Mama for inspection in what had become her sick room. Daddy was spending nights on the sleeping porch since her return. I was wearing the sailor dress I had worn the day of my baptism. As I twirled around for Mama my hand dove in the pocket and fished out the sword badge left there since that day. She pinned it to my collar, gave me a kiss of approval. I skipped happily through the door.

On the way to church Daddy said, "Children, I've got something important to tell you."

My eyes widened and I scooted to the edge of the seat.

"You may as well know I've been asked to resign as preacher." No one said a word. Parker and I exchanged surprised looks and I put a finger to my lips to indicate silence.

Daddy continued, "This morning during Sunday school they'll take a vote on whether I'm to stay. If I'm voted out, I'll just say a public farewell and we'll leave without me giving a sermon. I wanted y'all to know what's going on to avoid confusion, just in case."

Faye asked, "How can they just vote you out, Daddy?"

"That's just how it works. A preacher stays only as long as the congregation wants him. They pay my salary."

"But why wouldn't they want you anymore?" she asked.

"I'm afraid you're too young to understand." With that often-heard answer we rode the rest of the way in silence.

As we walked through the front doors I announced, "I'm not going to Sunday School."

"Oh, yes you are," said Gene. "You're too young for this too."

Faye hurried to where the primary children were bunched into classes at the back of the church. The adults were organizing in front. I marched right up behind my brothers and sat on the front pew next to Parker. My hands were trembling so I sat on them and swung my legs in and out from under the seat while I listened to everyone settling behind us.

Deacon Thompson protested at my presence, but Daddy looked at my determined face and shrugged. "Let her stay. I'm not ashamed for my children to hear what I have to say." He sat down on the other side of me.

Next, Deacon Hewitt rose to his feet. He spoke quietly and I noted a hint of sadness in his voice. "I am sorry to report it's been brought to my attention a grave impropriety may have occurred while Preacher Miller's good wife was in the hospital. As you're probably aware, Sister Loraine Schaefer was hired to take over the household duties. Now, we all try to help each other out during adversity, and this was certainly one of those times. I believe she was paid fairly for her domestic services." Perspiration formed on his forehead as he spoke and he tugged a handkerchief from his suit coat pocket and dabbed it before continuing.

"However, one of our sisters, who shall remain anonymous, approached me last week to say she had found evidence that the preacher and Miss Schaefer were closer than employer and employee and were,"—he looked over at me—"for lack of another polite word—intimate during Sister Miller's absence. This supposedly took place while the children were in the house."

A gasp burst from the congregation. I had no familiarity with the word "intimate" but I was worried at the way it was used. I cut my eyes up at Daddy but he was concentrating on the deacon.

"Deacon Thompson and myself went to the preacher's home last Thursday night to confront him with this accusation. He denied there was any truth to it, but said he would replace Miss Schaefer promptly, which I understand he's done. What remains now is for us to decide what we want to do about this."

Someone said, "Let's hear from the preacher."

"Yes," echoed another voice. "Let's hear Brother Miller's side."

Daddy rose and faced us. I twisted the tie on my dress and chewed on my lower lip.

He cleared his throat like he did before giving a sermon. "Brothers and sisters, I've been your pastor for four years now. I've rejoiced with you at your baptisms; I've cried with you over the loss of your loved ones. Our families have shared dinner together and spent many pleasant hours in one another's company. I feel like we ought to know me by now."

I felt myself being hypnotized. His tone of voice, the way he emphasized some words and whispered others, was leading me down memories of church picnics, last year's Christmas pageant, my own baptism. He was right. He had been there. Love and pride gushed through me. How could anyone doubt him? I gained strength from his words.

He walked over to me, picked up his Bible from the pew, and raised it high above his head. His voice rose to a shout: strong, sure, convincing. "I swear before Almighty God, on His most Holy Word, I've never shared a bed with Loraine

Schaefer." He paused and lowered his voice and I strained to hear him. "It grieves me that you would even think I'd do such a thing. God knows the truth, and I pray you'll find it in your hearts to believe me, for like innocent men before me, I stand wrongly accused." He had tears in his eyes as he sat down and placed the Bible reverently in his lap.

I stared at him in disbelief.

"Close your mouth," whispered Gene. He leaned over Parker and poked me in the ribs to get my attention. What's the matter with you?"

I couldn't answer. I couldn't speak. A tightness in my chest made it hard to breathe as the vision of Daddy and Loraine forced itself upon me.

My father encircled my shoulder with his arm and I shrank like a snake had slithered around me. He looked at me strangely and moved it to the back of the pew. Deacon Hewitt stood again. "In light of the fact we must feel free to discuss this and cast our ballots, I'd ask the preacher and his children to kindly leave the sanctuary. We'll call you back when we've reached a decision."

The family stood and headed for the door, except me. I was motionless. Gene came back and pulled me up by one limp arm. "Come on little sister," he said through clenched teeth and a fake smile. I felt weak and scared as he pulled me down the aisle and through the door.

They headed for the shade of a pine tree across the church yard but I stumbled away from them and crossed the road to a grove of dogwood trees. I sat down and hugged my knees. Squeezing my eyes shut, I tried not to think. When Gene came to tell me they were calling us back inside I didn't answer; I didn't care. I stayed there what seemed like forever until I thought surely, they should have come out and we should have left in shame and disgrace.

I pulled myself up and checked the church entrance. It was vacant and peaceful, the doors open to let in fresh air. All seemed quiet until I heard the piano begin the strains of "Footsteps of Jesus.' Curiosity overpowered me. I had to find out what was happening. Crossing the road and skirting around to the side of the building, I duck-walked under the first window and hurried to the one nearest the pulpit. Cautiously, I raised my head till my eyes were just above the sill. Daddy was in his usual place as if it were an ordinary Sunday. Would God strike him with lightning? I looked at the sky and searched for dark clouds. It was a pure baby blue, not a cloud in sight.

It was suddenly obvious what had happened. The Devil had hopped from Parker into Daddy because of him swearing on the Bible and telling a lie. What if he fell down and started foaming at the mouth like men in the New Testament who were suddenly possessed? It was too horrible to imagine. I dropped to my knees and crawled beyond the church, then began to run.

I took the worn path to the river. When I reached the water's edge I was panting. I stared at the spot where I'd been baptized and imagined it was mocking me. Was my baptism a lie too? Then I thought about Mama. Did she know? Should I tell her what happened? I wanted to jump in the river, but instead I searched around for something I could throw in. As I whirled around, the ribbon from the badge on my collar fluttered and caught my eye.

I grabbed the sword badge and yanked it. I heard a rip like a puppy yelp and tucked my chin under to see what had made the sound. A half-inch ragged tear on the sailor collar gaped up at me. Anger and regret leaped up in me and I clenched the pin, closing my hand into a fist. The point pierced my skin. A strange satisfaction came with the pain. I welcomed it. Furiously I ripped off the ribbons and flung them in the river. I clawed the silver paper off the sword, tore it into tiny scraps and hurled them onto the ground. I shredded the sword into so many bits it was unrecognizable, then threw myself, sobbing on top of the mutilated badge. I pounded the ground with my fist. I just wanted to die.

By the time Gene found me my tears were replaced with a hollow aching sadness. In hopes that Gene would put me out of my misery by killing me, I confessed everything, peeking through the keyhole and seeing Daddy in bed with Loraine. "Has God struck him dead? Did he start rolling around on the floor foaming at the mouth like Queenie did when she got rabies?" I thought of our beloved cocker spaniel who had become a glassy-eyed, vicious stranger that had to be "put down." I crossed my fingers in hopes that he hadn't.

"God isn't going to strike him dead." He hugged me and turned his face away. His voice sounded sort of shaky.

I looked at him. "Will he go to hell for this? I don't want him to burn in hell, no matter what he did."

Gene said, "I don't know if he'll go to hell or not, but just remember, you didn't do anything wrong; he did. And even though we know he lied, enough folks believed him that he wasn't kicked out of church. Besides, God has so many big sins to deal with like murder and war and stuff maybe he missed this one. I tell you what. It's going to be easier for God to forgive him than it will be for me. It'll be a cold day in hell before I forget what he did." His voice had a hard angry edge like the axe he used to cut the heads off chickens for Sunday dinner.

Wobbling to his feet, he held out his hand to help me up.

"Can you keep a secret?"

"Course I can," I answered, poking my chin up indignantly.

"We can't upset Mama about this. It's real important since she's been so sick. This thing has to be our secret. Promise?"

"Cross my heart and hope to die; stick a needle in my eye," I swore, and made an "X" over my heart.

"Come on, let's go home, he said.

"I have to do something first. Will you wait for me?"

"You bet."

I gathered up the remnants of the badge and walked to a sandy spot by the edge of the river. Kneeling, I dug a shallow hole, tenderly placed the pieces into it, and buried them under the sand.

Losing Zan Gambol

Cold. Silence. Coffin darkness.

A faint keening within and without. A siren. An ambulance slices through snow-ghosted mountains toward Champlain Valley Physicians Hospital like a pathologist's steel cutting cadaver.

Strapped, purged, I lie in the back. "Check her pockets. Sometimes they hide pills for later in case they don't succeed. Tape that IV in and take her shoes in case she tries to run when we get there."

11:45 p.m.

Arrival. Cargo at port. Transfer complete.

A white blur swoops at me flapping, squawking, "We need you to sign this admission form." I narrow my eyes. "No! Let me out of here!"

"I'll just write 'Involuntary'."

1:05 a.m.

"Taking up MH patient." Wheelchair trapped along corridors, up ramps, through automatic doors whooshing open, slamming shut. Psycho ward, loony bin, nut house. In the 21st century, politically correct Mental Health Unit. A desk. Nurse hisses orders, "Strip down to your underwear." Foists two rags in my chest. "Put one on back to front and the other front to back."

"It's not my color!"

"Here's a pair of socks to wear while you're on the ward." Yellow plastic bracelet melded on, numbered, labeled, making me easy to identify, if I ever escape from the locked ward, as a social pariah. *Oh my God! What if they won't let me out? Like him? Act normal. Make them realize this is a mistake, a misunderstanding.*

"Your shoes and other personal items will be placed in a locker with your name on it. If you need something, you must ask one of the staff for it."

Slam, click. My shoes are locked in their own tiny cell.

"Follow me," she snaps, and I sluggishly trail after her to a cramped room with a table and two chairs.

"Have a seat. I have to take some background." Without looking up, "Full name?" A litany of questions. I'm on autopilot until one.

"I said how many siblings?"

"Six. Well, five."

"Which is it?" she asks.

"Five. One died."

"Date of death?"

"Three weeks ago." I can hear my voice quivering. I don't want to think about this.

She's relentless. "Cause of death?" Her pen scratches information about Zan Gambol, staining his memory by ink-slinging him into this foul place. "Pneumonia is the 'official cause,' but that's just the last of their lies. They killed him."

She recoils. "Who killed him?"

"Quack doctors in a place just like this."

"And why do you think they would do something like that?"

"I don't think it; I *know* it. Twenty years of neglect and Thorazine. Just put that down. No. Change that to murder. That's the real reason." I jump up and begin pacing.

She abruptly stands up. "We can finish this tomorrow. You must be tired." Her sudden concern makes me suspicious.

I'm led to a room with a hungry camera. Cyclops eats my every move.

"Bathroom is there. You share it with the patient in the next room. Keep the door to your room open at all times. Breakfast is seven to eight in the morning. It is not brought to you. You have to go to the dining room."

Finally, alone, I curl into a question mark on the granite bed unable to sleep. Head is throbbing, throbbing. Wasn't it Jacob who was sleeping on stones and angels visited him in a dream? That's what they taught me in Sunday school. Daddy spent twenty years selling that crap to us. His *calling*. I have a few things I'd like to call him, if he were still alive.

Intermittently, footsteps approach, recede. Think ocean, warm sand, waves rolling over my toes. Instead, a vision pops into my mind of Anne Frank shackled to her bed by fear that footsteps she hears might be Nazis. After two years locked in that tiny attic, they got her anyway.

I need to go to the bathroom, but am frightened of meeting the lunatic next door. I close my eyes again. It hits me with such force I can hardly breathe: The memory of that first visit to Zan Gambol. It pulses through me like the drugs I've ingested.

Zan Gambol, my favorite older brother, had been chucking peanut shells at a Leghorn rooster to make him crow. That was the last time I saw him before he disappeared.

Eight months later we were reunited on a stifling July day. Perched on the hump seat between Paul Thomas and Vera, my next older brother and sister, we slid around the twisted drive of Dorothea Dix State Hospital for the Mentally Ill in Raleigh.

I was scared to death to see Zan Gambol. I had thought about him every day since he disappeared. What if he didn't remember me? Or what if he had turned into a kind of monster so I wouldn't know him? I had a headache from worrying about it.

The sharp curves, combined with the heat, sent a wave of nausea over me. I flopped against Paul Thomas when we swerved left and he jabbed me in the side with his boney elbow.

"Mother! I feel sick, and P.T.'s pokin' me."

P.T. snapped, "Shut up, you big baby!"

Daddy slammed on the brakes and the car lurched forward and back. He turned around and gritted his teeth. "I told you to behave back there. Isn't this hard enough without you making trouble? You're just daring me, aren't you boy?"

"No, sir," P.T. answered.

Before P.T. could duck, Daddy backhanded him on the head. "If I hear one more word out of you, you won't be able to sit down for a week! You hear me?"

P.T. nodded, blinked hard and rubbed his head. He never cried when Daddy hit him.

A sudden stinging in the back of my throat and a rush of saliva was a signal for me to move fast. I yelled, "I'm gonna throw up!" I climbed over Vera and jumped out of the car and threw up in the grass.

Mother appeared beside me and dabbed my chin. She held onto me while I vomited again, then handed me the top of a Thermos brimming with water. "Rinse your mouth out and take a deep breath. Try and swallow these aspirins."

I did as I was told. "I didn't mean for P.T. to get hit."

"Ssshh. I know. You feeling better since you got sick? Sometimes that eases the pain."

I nodded weakly and struggled back into the car. We continued up the twisted road to the top of hill.

Daddy pulled into a parking space in the stringy shade of a mimosa tree and went in the Administration Building. When he was out of ear shot, I looked at P.T., who was staring out the window. "I'm sorry. I didn't know he would do that."

He looked at me with something close to hate. "Then you must be stupid as well as ugly."

Mother turned around in the front seat. "Hush that kind of talk now, P.T. He's just worried about your brother. You know you shouldn't push him."

"Why don't y'all get out and wait under that tree."

Instantly we were out of the car. P.T. dared me to climb the tree. My headache was easing a little so I started up, figuring I'd get a good view of the hospital grounds, not caring if everybody on the ground could get a perfect view of my underwear. Mother grabbed me by one lacy anklet and told me that was no way for a lady to behave, especially in a dress.

"But you made me wear a dress! It's not my fault."

She had scolded me numerous times that it wasn't proper for young ladies to act like boys; that there were certain things I had to accept to get along in this world and my place was not competing with every boy who dared me to do something.

Daddy came towards us and pointed to a sprawling, squatty building.

"He's over yonder."

I stared, absorbing every detail of where my brother spent his time till he could come home. It looked different than the other buildings around. There were no trees to shelter it, making it bare and lonely looking. On the left, barbed wire jailed a hard-packed, dusty yard with a parched grass fringe. A rusty basketball hoop sagged from a weathered post at one end.

I thought how much Zan Gambol would hate being penned in. All last summer he and I headed out after supper, when he'd finished in the tobacco field, and wandered the woods and creeks. Sometimes we pretended we were soldiers searching for the enemy; sometimes we were the enemy. Once we crawled under the fence between our land and Fort Bragg's to see the soldiers training in war games. We never told a soul about it or he'd have been skinned alive. We knew how to keep secrets.

3:10 a.m.

Light leaks through the open doorway so I can't sleep. I struggle up and close the door. Moments later it is flung open. A voice crashes over me. "This door is to stay open at all times; is that clear?"

I can't decide if it's a rhetorical question. Who the hell does that bitch think she is? I have the urge to slap her.

Her silhouette glows in the semidarkness, like an eel that slithered out of the sea into my room. I stare at her in wonder and loathing. If I close my eyes, I bet I can make her go away.

When I open my eyes, she *has* disappeared. I tiptoe to the bathroom door and listen. I'd rather meet the crazies out in the open. All is quiet so I step inside. There is no lock on either entry door. No shower curtain over the tub. Weak with naked vulnerability I quickly relieve myself.

In a rush I draw in my breath. Black urine. Must be from the charcoal they pumped into my stomach. Even my bodily functions have been invaded. I can't even pee in private.

1963

As I trudged towards Zan Gambol's building, the sun hammered down. Sweat pooled in my armpits. Mother had forced me to wear my black patent shoes that trapped the heat in the soles of my feet, and I wondered if walking on hot tar could be any worse. I was itching to pull them off so my feet could breathe and cool me down.

I followed the others through the screen door and observed a desk set at a right angle. A man behind it looked up from a yellowed paperback and scrambled to his feet. He had skin partly white with splatters of brown along one cheek sliding into the collar of his shirt. I stared and wondered if he had one colored parent and it was God's punishment to make him come out two-toned.

"Hey there, folks. It's a scorcher out there today, hain't it," Daddy said in a voice reserved for strangers.

The man flicked his thumb at a rotating fan on his desk as he set the book face down. "This feels like hit's breathin' fire, but I reckon hit's better'n nothin'."

As I peered at him from behind Mother, he took a paper out of the middle drawer and snapped a pen from his shirt pocket.

"Who'd y'all come to visit?"

Daddy cleared his throat and said awkwardly, "Zan Gambol Miller, my middle boy." He shoved his hands in his pockets, walked to the door with his back to us, and stared out, humming some hymn to himself while the man talked with Mother and wrote our names and ages on a form.

"Glad to see Zan gettin' visitors, but I'm afraid you have to be twelve to go into the secure ward. It's not a place for young 'uns, ma'am," he said apologetically to Mother. "The little 'un can stay out here. I'll keep an eye on her."

Mother knelt down and looked into my eyes. "Honey, it's probably best we see him first anyway; it's been so long. I'll tell him you're here and maybe he can come out and see you for a little while." A familiar stinging assaulted my eyes and I blinked hard, desperately trying to stop tears that threatened my dignity. They ignored me and flowed down my cheeks.

She handed me a tissue from her purse. "It'll be all right. This nice man will be here if you need anything while we're gone."

I clung to her wrist to keep her from leaving me alone. "It smells bad".

"That's just ammonia. All hospitals use that to keep down germs. You'll be fine." She led me to a wooden bench along the wall.

The man picked up a telephone on the desk and moments later I watched my family follow another uniformed man through a gate of iron bars that slid open at the turn of his key and then slammed shut behind them. It was a hard, empty sound that made me feel so lonesome I cried even harder.

"Now, don't be like that," Splotchy said. "How 'bout if I get you a soda pop? Would you like that?"

His question reminded me that I needed to go to the bathroom. Between sniffles I managed a "No, thank you."

He shrugged, flipped the book over and resumed reading "The Last Trail".

The waiting room was uglier than the halls at Long Branch Elementary School. The floor was gray tiles, the walls a dirty color like Scooter Gant, a boy in my class, who looked like he never took a bath. Scratched wooden benches, like the one I sat on, were stuck along two walls. Windows on either side of the front door were screened and had wire mesh bolted on the inside, I guess to prevent kids under twelve breaking in. A Royal Crown Cola calendar with the year torn off hung above the desk where Splotchy sat dozing, his patchy face bobbing on one shoulder.

My eyes wandered around the room when a sign grabbed my attention with the words *Rest Rooms* and an arrow. I started jiggling up and down. I wasn't sure what was more terrifying, wetting my pants or going to the bathroom in a crazy house where I could catch crazy germs from the toilet seat or maybe even from the faucet handles of the sink. I crossed my legs and scrunched them together, and tried to think of something else.

Darting a quick glance at the sleeping man, I wriggled off the bench and tiptoed around the corner. There was a short, dead-end hallway with two doors. Thankfully *Ladies* was first. I slowly tugged on the door.

I scooted inside. Keeping the door open in case I had to make a quick getaway, I stood listening for crazy people that might be inside. Hearing nothing but the drip-drip of a faucet, I opened the second swinging door where three stalls yawned along the right-hand wall across from the sinks. I drew my breath in as a woman whirled around from a small meshed window opposite me.

I knew the sign on the door hadn't said "Colored Women", and I was so stunned to see her I was confused for several seconds and just stood there.

She blew smoke between a dark funnel of lips. "Hey there."

I caught sight of a gold tooth gleaming like a kernel of corn. "Hey," I answered and quickly ducked into the first stall and locked the door with trembling fingers. Careful not to sit on the seat, since I now had to also worry about colored germs, I went while humming "Dixie" to cover the embarrassing sound. When I finished, I took as long as possible, hoping the woman had left.

Slowly, I unlocked the door and looked to my right. She was still there. I glanced away and hurried to the sink to wash my hands. "You got a daddy or brother in here?"

I eyed her warily. My pulse thrummed in my ears when I noticed she had a name tag on her blouse. I tried to remember if Splotchy had a name tag, attempting to put her in the crazy or not crazy category.

"I'm not supposed to talk to strangers," I replied, yanking a paper towel from the dispenser.

The woman burst out laughing. To my horror, she approached and loomed over me. I jumped back against the wall but there was no protection from her crazy (had to be) germs.

"He must be real bad to get locked away in this here McBride building."

In spite of fear my temper flared. I stared straight into her bottomless dark eyes. "My brother is not bad! My folks say it's nobody's business why he's here." I was shaking with fury.

She glared down, refusing to move back. "The days when sassy little white girls tell grown women what to do are over, child. That temper what got your brother locked up in here?" The woman laughed again, a high, squealing sound that made the hair on the back of my neck stand up. I pushed past her and ran out as fast as I could, through the waiting room, straight to the car. I jumped in, locked the doors, rolled up the windows, wrapped my arms around myself and lay there in the heat, hiding, trembling all over, sweat pouring off me. I felt like a lightning bug trapped in a jar, unable to get enough air. I promised myself it would be the last time I would catch any without letting them go again.

7:50 a.m.

A cart rattles in the distance. People shuffle by in socks and slippers. Okay. I'm not hungry, but I've got to scope out my surroundings, plan my escape.

The cart is down the hall a dozen yards to my right. I pass the nurses' station, television monitors suspended over the desk. Two nurses are engaged in conversation. At the doorway to the dining room, I hesitate.

A few sleepy-eyed people look up so I quickly avert my eyes. Others seem to be communing with their breakfasts. The only empty chair is next to a stocky man, sixtyish, sipping from a Styrofoam cup. Cautiously I slip into it. A foil covered tray in front of me has a place card with my name on it. A crushing weight descends on me. I want to pick the tray up and hurl it through the air. *I* don't belong here!

From where I'm sitting, the door to the ward is visible. A button perches to the right that sounds a buzzer when hospital staff come and go.

"I said give it back!" A man at the next table is yelling at a woman. She leaps up, pulls her arm back and shoves his tray onto the floor.

"You bitch!" He lurches toward her, knocking over his chair. A commanding voice orders everyone to their rooms.

Prickly heat stings my underarms. Everyone is preoccupied. The timing is perfect. I duck into the hall past the food cart where a wild-looking man in skewed pajamas is jamming an empty tray into a metal slot. I look over my shoulder. The man who was sitting next to me looks at me and barks like a dog.

I push the buzzer to release the door, ram my shoulder against it. It bursts open. I run like hell. Careering into a corridor on my left, fifty feet ahead is the door to freedom. I crush the bar latch.

Freezing air slaps me, rushes into my lungs. Snow bites into my socks and sends a shock wave through my body. A shelter of evergreens beckons on my left. I sprint across the parking lot towards it. The hospital gown flaps like loose skin. With adrenaline pumping through me, ahead I see a stubborn mound of snow clinging to the base of a light post. Hearing people yelling at me from behind, I'm forced to jump it. My chest aches. One lane in the empty parking lot now separates me from the trees.

The next instant I'm three feet down. Can't catch my breath. A massive weight is smothering me. My face, hands, knees, are forced into snow-plowed, icy asphalt. Sickening sweet blood oozes onto my tongue. I can't move. I struggle, scream. "Get off me, you fucking bastard! Let me go!" I'm yelling down into the ground like I'm screaming at the devil.

Arms grabbed, crisscrossed over my stomach. Encased in a padded vest cinched at the back, I kick and kick again. "Let me go! You can't keep me here!"

Well-trained thugs, they jerk my ankles into cuffs, then hoist and haul me back to the ward. Its mouth slams shut. I'm swallowed whole. Jonah. A nurse rushes toward us. "Everyone back in your rooms." People stare from doorways like *I'm* the freak.

They drag me into my room. A nurse and another man appear. Between them and the guards, they unlock the cuffs, grab my ankles and tether them to the bed. They remove the straitjacket, then yank me to a sitting position, grab my arms, and tie them to opposite sides of the bed in four-point restraint. The men leave me alone with the nurse.

Consumed with fury, I want to smash her face in.

"Calm down. We're not going to hurt you."

I begin shaking with cold and terror. My nose is running, but I can't wipe it. Soon it will be stopped up. I turn my head and try to rub it on the pillow.

The nurse's voice is quiet, sneaky. She holds a tissue to my nose as if I'm a toddler. "Blow." Dabs at my abrasions with a cloth. "Close your eyes. This is an antiseptic spray to keep down infection."

I obey.

A blanket appears and she covers me. "You'll have to stay like this for a few hours and then we can let you up, if you promise not to run away again." She walks toward the door, then turns. "I'm sorry this had to be done. We're just trying to help you. When you're better – and you will get better – you'll realize it was necessary."

1963

Mother banged on the car window with her palm. "Sugar, open the door! Zan Gambol is coming out to see you." Overjoyed to see her, I bolted up and unlocked the door. "What in heaven's name are you doing locked in the car like this? Did that man say something to upset you?"

I shook my head, deciding not to tell her what had happened. Avoiding her question, I asked, "What's he look like? Is he changed much?"

"No. He looks the same. Maybe a little thinner. But he's still the same brother who cuddled you. He's anxious to see you. Come on."

I crawled out of the car and stayed on Mother's heels up the hill. Once inside, my eyes swiveled toward the corner leading to the bathroom, but there was no sign of the crazy woman.

Daddy, Vera, and P.T. sat against the far wall of the waiting room. When they saw us, they headed outside. Vera squeezed my arm when she passed, as if to say it was going to be all right.

Zan Gambol, wearing a gray shirt and pants, was waiting at the barred hallway with a uniformed man not far away. He grasped the bars like a prisoner. Mother saw me hesitate and gently pushed me towards him.

I smoothed my hair unconsciously and then my damp, wrinkled dress. I ran to him and grabbed his hands.

"Hey Kitten," he said, grinning. He measured the top of my head by his hand against his chest. "You sure have got tall. How old are you now?"

"Eight my last birthday. Mother says I'm growin' like a weed." I studied him and blurted out, "What happened to your teeth?"

He opened his mouth wide, showing me pink, bumpy gums where his front teeth used to be. As if remembering a dream, his eyes got a faraway look. "A guard down Florida decided I could do without them."

"He made you get 'em pulled?"

He leaned forward and whispered, "I ran away and they come after me with bloodhounds. When they caught me, one of them whacked me in the face with a club. I was fighting 'em trying to get away. Awww now, don't cry. Please. It ain't that bad. You don't see me cryin' over it."

He looked out the front door where the rest of the family had disappeared. "Everybody looks the same. Everything all right at home? How's your dog? I forget his name."

"Rusty," I said, remembering the way his whole body wagged with joy into a giant "C" to a "J" when I came home from school, how I used to bury my cheek in his thick, yellow fur. "Daddy took him out in the woods one day and I never saw him again. I swear I thought I heard a shot, but I couldn't tell whether it came from the army camp or not. I think Daddy shot him."

He scratched his head absentmindedly. "How come he done that?"

"You know how he warned me to keep him away from the chickens? One day he got out. Killed two of Daddy's prize, barred rock hens."

The questions I had bottled up came tumbling out. "Where'd you go? What were you doin' in Florida?"

He looked surprised, then chuckled deep and crazy-like. "Don't you know?"

"No. Every time I asked Mother she got upset, so I quit askin'. I've been worried sick about you. You look skinny."

"Yeah. Lost weight down at the prison."

My eyes grew scared big. "You were in prison?"

"Yeah. They feed you all right here, though, but I could use some candy. Ain't had a Baby Ruth since I got locked up. Remember when we'd walk through the woods to that old man's store to buy Baby Ruths and Grape Nehis?"

"Yeah, I remember. But go on with your story." I patted his hands. Sometimes it was hard to keep his mind on track. "What happened the day you disappeared? The last thing I knew Vera rushed onto the porch and grabbed me by the hand. We took off runnin' and hid in the tobacco barn. "I guess I got beat pretty bad that time. All I remember is lyin' in the back seat with Mother while Parker drove to the hospital. From there I went to some boys' home. Me and…"

I gasped. "How long were you in the hospital?"

"I don't remember. Anyways, me and two other boys run away from the home. Clay stole a car and drove all the way to Florida. Got to see palm trees and ocean. We got picked up by the state police below Jacksonville. They put me in a juvenile home, but I run away, so they locked me up in Raeford Prison. I don't want to think about that. It was real bad. I don't remember a lot about what happened there. I just woke up here one day."

I tried to take in all he was telling me, but it seemed unreal, like something on television.

I examined the lines in his forehead, ran my fingers over them. "Did you turn sixteen or seventeen on your birthday this year?"

"I can't remember. Ain't thought about it since I been locked up. Don't matter no how. Nobody gives you a birthday cake where I been." He sniggered like he'd told a funny joke. I stared at him, his shoulders shaking with strange laughter like a crazy person, and despite the heat, I felt something icy cold, like a claw, take hold of my insides.

He patted his shirt pocket searching for a cigarette. He found one, then raised it along with his eyebrows into a question at the guard, who waggled his finger no. Zan Gambol put it back. I wondered how come the guard could smoke but my brother couldn't.

Zan Gambol shoved his hands in his pockets and dug at the floor with one shoe. "Sometimes I get to thinkin' about what we used to do down home. Remember you sat on my lap and read me funny books, and I always wanted you to read westerns, but you wanted to read Little Lulu; you remember that?"

I nodded, not thinking of reading but of rubbing Vick's salve into welts on his back from Daddy's belt.

A happy memory jumped to mind and I smiled. "Remember how you would push me in the swing and I tried to touch the dogwood blossoms with my toes?"

"Yeah. You loved to go real high."

"I always knew you'd catch me if I fell."

Looking at him now, I couldn't imagine how I had thought that; he looked so weak and timid next to the smoking guard leaning against the far wall. I shivered involuntarily and squeezed his hands."

"When you comin' home?"

"They won't tell me."

"I sure miss you. All Vera wants to do now is try on make-up and talk about boys all the time. Says she's too old to play. And P.T.'s too mean. I want you to come home so we can do stuff together like we used to, just you and me. We always had so much fun."

He grinned a wide, snaggletooth grin.

I chewed on my lip. "Why are you locked up?"

"They think I'll run away." He leaned forward and whispered, "I would too. I'd get as far away from here as I could. Go out west and be a cowboy."

I stared at the guard who was approaching. "What you telling her, boy? Don't be scaring that little girl now. That won't do you no good. You know that."

Zan Gambol looked at the guard and laughed drily, a sound I'd never heard him make. "Boss, I ain't tellin' her nothin', but I miss her and rememberin' the games we used to play. She's my baby sister."

The guard looked at me and smiled. "Is that a fact? You related to this rascal?"

"Yes, sir," I said respectfully, knowing instinctively he had Zan Gambol under his control.

"What's your name?" he asked.

Zan Gambol answered before I could. "April. Ain't she cute as a button?"

The man seemed to study me and said, "She's a beauty. How'd such an ugly cuss like you have such a pretty sister?"

Zan Gambol shook his head, and with a silly grin said, "I don't know, Boss."

I didn't find the man's remark the least bit funny. Zan Gambol and I had the same green eyes and freckles, same wavy red hair. The guard's words stung like a switch on bare legs. I didn't know what to say, but I felt compelled to defend my brother. I blurted out, "Folks always say we look alike."

He seemed to accept that as the last word and walked away without comment. I didn't add that when Daddy got mad at me, he'd yell, "You're just like your crazy brother!"

I beckoned Zan Gambol to come closer while the guard's back was turned. I whispered, "We could go out West together. Live on a ranch like Roy Rogers and Dale Evans. We could even have our own horses. Oh, let's do it! What can I do to help you escape?"

He leaned back and shook his head. "I'll have to think about that one. I'll let you know next time you come to visit. I sure wish we all could be together again, though. I miss y'all, especially you." He changed the subject abruptly. "Would you ask Mother to bring me a carton of Camels next time y'all come? And a transistor radio if she can. I sure would like that. It'd help pass the time if I could listen to Elvis." He started singing off key, "You ain't nothin' but a hound dog, cryin' all the time…" Do you think I sound like him?"

Startled out of the western daydream, I nodded, not knowing what else to say.

The guard approached again and tapped him on the shoulder. "Zan, it's time to take you back. Y'all wind it up now."

I couldn't say goodbye. I didn't know when I'd see him again. A knot in my stomach made me want to scream and hit the man until he let my brother go. Zan Gambol reached his hand through the bars and petted my face. I grabbed it, trying to keep the feel of his calluses, his familiar tobacco smell. He turned and hunched his shoulders like a tired old man as the guard took his arm and led him away. I watched him grow smaller and finally disappear.

Clutching the bars, a cry rose from a cold, dark place inside me. It got louder, wilder, until I was sealed off, suspended in space and time. I sensed, rather than heard, people running behind me, but I hung there, unable to move until someone pried my fingers off. I shrieked over and over, "Zan Gambol! Come back!" But he didn't come back, and the screams echoed and died down the long empty corridor.

Good Intentions

"Has anyone seen Beryl?" Anne Minton swiped gray, wispy bangs off her forehead. "I haven't seen a trace of her in over a week." Like an activated sprinkler, the question sprayed cold water on a circle of neighbors at a St. Patrick's Day gathering hosted by Ed and Mary Rooney. Guests looked at one another, shrugged, or shook their heads. Though not unusual to miss neighbors dashing in and out during months of snow and ice, someone should have seen her puttering in her yard after the recent thaw.

Katie and Todd van Heusen had recently moved to Blue Haven. Like in any small town, news blew through the village like a brisk wind that the couple was from New York City and were expecting their first child. They had bought the cozy vintage house directly across from Beryl's. Chatting with Katie earlier that evening, Anne asked if she knew whether the baby was a girl or boy.

Katie patted her baby bump and smiled. "We don't know yet, but we're planning a reveal party later this spring."

Ed handed Katie sparkling water with lime. What do you think of the woman who lives in that eyesore at number 12?"

"I find her pleasant. I think it's rather fun having our own eccentric on the street. She's odd but her presence is a reminder that not everyone is as well off as those of us who can afford lawn service and other amenities to keep our homes from decay. It's a reality check, don't you think?" Her face slid into a wry smile.

Taking time to temper his response, Ed growled under his breath as if clearing his throat.

His lower lip curled down, and he rolled his eyes. "The derelict property negatively affects our property values."

Beryl's property was a blight in the middle of the block, making her a frequent subject of conversation. One neighbor made an anonymous complaint to the code enforcement officer to report that the property created a hazard due to large, decayed trees that should be removed. Nothing came of it. Anne suspected it was Ed, since he seemed to bring the subject up every time she saw him. She found his insults to her neighbor rude, even misogynistic.

Anne and her sister, Gail, had moved onto the street three years earlier to be closer to town. One day early on, while collecting branches and twigs fallen from overhanging trees on Beryl's side of the shared, rickety fence, they had met their neighbor. Anne warmed to her spirit of calm. Peeping out from a green, floppy hat, Beryl mentioned how much she loved the wildflowers that persisted among the ever-present ivy. Despite the inconvenience Beryl's naturalist proclivities caused her regarding the trees, she observed her neighbor's multiple missing teeth, which signaled she must be destitute. That explained the condition of the property. Anne clicked her tongue, thinking, there but for the grace of God and my sister…

In fine weather, Beryl often darted among the trees and underbrush, her green hat like a rare nesting bird. Anne had noted that no one visited Beryl, at least by car. She and Anne had agreed between themselves to keep a lookout for her. Like enthusiastic bird watchers, they routinely informed one another if either had made a sighting. Occasionally, they passed her on a bicycle, paper bags fluttering from a carryall behind the seat.

The previous November, a sign was posted in Beryl's front yard that the property would be auctioned in the coming months. Upon seeing it, Anne rushed inside to tell Gail, who was rolling out a pastry for shepherd's pie, looked up. "I'll bet the bank has threatened to foreclose on her house. She must not have enough money to pay her taxes."

"The poor woman. You're probably right. I heard from someone that she has a slew of kids scattered across the state. You'd think they'd help out."

Before the auction date, the sign was removed. Rumor on the block was that the children had come to her rescue, a consensus being they probably paid it because none of them wanted her to live with them.

One neighbor secretly hoped she would be in a nursing home or gone before he had to sell his house, convinced the blight on the neighborhood depressed property values.

By the time snow shrank to dirty, misshapen towers, Beryl usually moved her bicycle from its winter storage to the side porch. Anne had not seen Beryl nor the bike. This had given rise to her question.

Jason Patterson, who lived in the house south of Beryl, tried to remember when he had last seen her. A mild-mannered man, he was rarely ruffled by affairs of neighbors. In his late forties and possessing a sensitive air, he directed another question to the gathering. "Are you suggesting someone should go over there for a safety check?"

Longtime resident Louise Winthrop pursed her lips and shook her head, bringing attention to its white, stationary helmet of hair that defied nature. Louise waved a hand back and forth. "That would be a waste of time. She won't answer the door. Like I told the sisters, she never does."

Matt O'Donoghue, a beefy, seasoned volunteer of the local fire department, paused in the middle of regaling friends with one of his stories. Stroking his Viking-worthy copper beard, he dislodged flakes from several bite-size spanakopita he'd popped into his mouth between sentences. "If there's a question of her safety, I could check it out. Louise, since you know her, what do you think? I don't know anything about the woman except what I've heard."

Louise wrinkled her nose beneath thick glasses and peered at the bouquet of faces in the family room. "Where's Angie?"

A confident voice lifted above the crowd. "Over here." Angie, a sturdy woman who delivered the mail, said, "Sorry. I can't help you. I rarely see her in winter, though sometimes she opens the door to say hello. Come to think of it, I can't remember when I last saw her, but that's not unusual. There's a mail slot in the door, so I don't know if her mail has been piling up."

Whispers bubbled like a steamy cauldron spewing a sense of foreboding. To gain control of runaway rumors, Ed sauntered to an arched doorway between the dining and family rooms. He raised his arms like an orchestra conductor. "Friends, settle down." A partner in a busy accounting firm, he was used to giving orders. Within moments, silence zippered the chatter. "I don't believe there's any reason to be alarmed. As I see it, we have several options. We can do nothing and assume she's holed up in her house for whatever reason, or someone can go over there and knock on the door, explain neighbors are worried about her and need to make sure she's okay."

Mary said, "Where are her children? I assume they talk to her by phone, but I don't really know. Does anyone know if they check on her?"

Louise spiraled through the crowd to the hosts and turned to face everyone. "I've lived here longer than most of you. As for the kids and their relationship with Beryl, that's a complicated story, which I won't get into. Concerning whether one of us ought to check on her, if you decide to do that, I think you should wait till daylight before going onto that property. You'll frighten the poor woman half to death because no one ever goes over there during the day, much less at night—except Angie, of course. She's a very private person. I don't see any reason to go sticking our noses in her business.

"If you insist, two of you could go there in the morning, but with all the rusted junk in the yard, you could get hurt stumbling around over there in the dark. Another night isn't going to make any difference." A consensus was reached. Jason and Matt volunteered to go to Beryl's the following morning.

At the agreed time, the men turned into a remnant of a driveway to Beryl's house. It was one of the oldest homes in the village, dating to the early 1800s. Set in an acre of land, the wooded lot had returned to its natural state over time. Skirting saplings struggling for light beside tall evergreens, they approached the front. Jason sensed an aura of emptiness, even sadness hanging about the place as he searched for bicycle tracks in shallow, muddy puddles leading to the sagging stoop. None were evident.

They stopped short at the front steps, which had rotted out over the winter. Matt shook his head and frowned. "That's not a good sign."

Continuing along the right to a side entrance, a screened porch leaned precariously towards the disused drive as if preparing to sprint away from the dilapidated house. Jason stooped to look under the porch. "I found her bike. She must be home."

Matt tugged on the screen door, which had warped shut. Once inside the porch, he crossed to the entrance and banged loudly. "Ms. Grant? Are you in there? It's Matt O'Donoghue from the fire department." After several attempts to draw her out to no avail, he bent to look through the mail slot. Unable to see in the poor light within, he stepped to the window right of the door. Heavy plastic sheeting attached to the frame on the inside obscured the interior. He proceeded to a second window further down with the same result.

"I can't see a thing. Why don't you go around back and see if you can see inside, and I'll stay here in case she comes to the door? I don't think she's home."

Near the back of the two-story house, Jason wrangled heavy, evergreen boughs growing so close to the structure that the trunk had buckled the crumbling stone foundation. Chunks of mortar littered the soft ground beneath the tree, carpeted with soft needles shed over many years. Branches scratched his face as he pushed through and saw the remains of what he thought might be a root cellar. A sagging, open door allowed him to poke his head into semi-darkness. "Beryl, It's Jason from next door." The only sound was the wind soughing through the tree.

Struggling out, he wound to the far side of the house where a ladder lay propped against a window. After testing it for weight-bearing, he climbed up. A slick layer of mildew clung to the outside sill. Inside, newspapers and garbage bags, cardboard boxes, and sundry items stacked to the ceiling bowed in and out like canyon cliffs. "What in the world?" he said aloud. He scrambled down and headed out to find Matt, whom he met rounding the corner of the house.

"Any luck?" Jason asked.

"Not a peep. I don't think she's here."

"You're not going to believe what I saw inside. Follow me." Jason pivoted and retraced his steps. "See for yourself."

Matt tentatively climbed the ladder. Pressing his face close to the window, he absorbed the implications of the mess inside. "Holy shit! Some of that may have fallen on her! I'm going in." Glancing down at Jason, he asked, "You coming?"

"Hold on a minute! Let's talk about this. That's against the law, Matt. If she's home and calls the police, we could be arrested."

Matt paused to consider. Patting his gloves together and already in rescue mode, he reached to open the window. "I think we should go in. She could be lying hurt somewhere in there."

"I'm not comfortable with that. It's breaking and entering. From the looks of it, she's been collecting this stuff for years, so there's no reason to believe she's not inside going about her business. Just peeping through her windows is an invasion of privacy. I'm not convinced we should even call the police at this point, but I'll concede we could and let them decide."

Matt cocked his head to one side. "Now that you mention it, what if she's away? There are no footprints or bike tracks. On the other hand, if she's lying injured underneath a pile of newspapers, and whatever the hell that other shit is, and can't call for help, maybe we could save her life."

Jason reasoned that there was no indication that she was home. "The question that began this whole thing was a question had anyone seen her. Just because no one had doesn't mean anything is wrong. Who asked the question anyway?"

"I'm not sure."

"It's my opinion things got out of control pretty fast. Keep in mind most of us were drinking. Maybe we let the situation get blown out of proportion. I live next door, and though I haven't seen her, I haven't seen the neighbors on the other side of me either. So, what's the rush to break into her house?"

Matt sighed. "That was before we knew about the Leaning Towers of Pisa in her house. She's a hoarder, and there's garbage, and who knows what everywhere."

"The point is we don't know that she's not perfectly fine. I think we should go home and keep an eye out for evidence that she's here and all right."

"Okay. I'll go along with you for a few days. I guess you're right; we should call the police to check it out." Matt's heart rate slowed along with his breathing.

"Good. Let's touch base in two or three days."

They hurried back to the front, where Jason cut across the yard to his house. On his way home, Matt stopped by Rooneys', who had volunteered to be the information center for concerned neighbors waiting for news of the visit to Beryl's and told them what had transpired.

The next three evenings, when Jason got home from work, he walked Sadie, his King Charles spaniel, past Beryl's. No lights shone in the house, and no bike tracks were visible.

Temperatures plummeted below freezing, and snow was forecast overnight. Everyone on Maple Street withdrew to the warmth of hearth and home, like rabbits in cozy dens.

It snowed all the next day. After dark, Anne squinted at Beryl's windows, trying to determine if a light was on. "Gail, can you have a look?" Gail answered, "I thought I saw lights on last night. "But it could have been a reflection of headlights on the windows."

Turning away from the window, Anne said, "Or maybe she's home. I'll bake some muffins and take over a plate; what do you think?"

Gail looked up from her book. "That's a nice idea. I'll go over with you. Between the two of us, maybe we can coax her to come to the door. Miracles do happen." Anne chuckled as Gail stretched out her arm with fingers crossed.

That evening, the sisters tugged on coats and winter paraphernalia and trekked through the snow to Beryl's house with muffins warm from the oven. There were no footprints in the new snow, Anne commented. Pulling off one glove, she pounded on the side door and shouted. "Beryl! It's your next-door neighbors. We brought you some muffins. Come get 'em while they're hot!" No sound drifted from inside. Gail walked to the far window porch and peered in. "I don't see any lights. She might be too far away to hear us. Maybe she's upstairs or watching tv, or she's not here."

Anne tried the door and shrugged. "I doubt she even has a tv. A radio, maybe. If we leave these on the porch overnight, you know animals will be thrilled. Oh, heck, may as well." She sighed and left the foil-covered paper plate on the threshold. They hurried back to the warmth of their house, each wondering if Beryl had returned and, if so, would she find the muffins before wildlife pounced on the unexpected feast. Anne headed straight for the bookshelf in the living room and retrieved the village phone directory. Thumbing through, she found the number for B. Grant and pressed the number to a landline. The phone rang multiple times. Unable to leave a message, she turned to Gail, who was in the recliner reading on her phone. "Well, looks like it was a waste of time to make those muffins."

Gail looked at Anne, the color draining from her face. "What do you mean? Has something happened?"

"I just called her number and let it ring off the hook. There was no answer. She's away or..." the sentence died on her lips. The two locked eyes thinking similar dark thoughts.

Angie ascended the steps at Beryl's house and shoved mail through the door slot. Glancing down to her right, she noticed a paper plate peeking out from the receding snow. Moving it with the toe of her boot, she determined it was empty. *Beryl must be feeding the animals again. The only problem is scraps attract all manner of animals, including rats. I don't think the neighbors would be thrilled about that,* she mused as she trudged to the sisters' house with a handful of catalogs. They received more than anyone on the block, and the added weight mad' her bag much heavier. She tried not to hold it against them, as they were friendly and always spoke to her. One bitterly cold day, they had offered her a cup of hot chocolate, which she was grateful for.

Jason intended to call Matt on Friday if he hadn't seen Beryl and suggest one of them call the police. When he and Sadie, his King Charles spaniel, walked past Beryl's on Thursday evening, he observed footprints to and from the house. Reassured, Jason breathed a sigh of relief that all had returned to normal, even though no lights were visible inside Beryl's house. Upon returning from the walk, he pushed his snowblower next door and cleared a path from Beryl's porch to the street, with a niggle of annoyance that she did not come out to thank him.

Matt passed by the next day and saw the cleared path. He said to his golden retriever, "I see the hoarder is back. We won't have to bust in there, after all, Buddy."

On Sunday night, Louise packed for a flight to California to visit her daughter. Mary Rooney drove her to the city airport, and on the way, conversation eventually turned to Beryl. Louise fidgeted with the purse in her lap. "You know, Mary, I'm a bit concerned that I still haven't seen Beryl. It's been almost a week since your party, and there's no sign of her."

Mary responded lightly, "Oh, I think she's there. After the storm, her path was cleared of snow."

Louise turned to look at her. "Still, it's odd that I haven't seen her. Sometimes she stays with her friend Barbara Fletcher on Sycamore Street. They go back a long way and sometimes stay with each other when one of them is ill. I don't think Beryl's ever stayed there more than a day or two. She likes to be home. It might be a good idea if someone gets in touch with Barbara, just to check. I would have done it if I'd thought about it earlier."

Mary loosened her grip on the steering wheel. "I don't know Barbara, but if you think they might be together, it makes me feel better." Her next thought was *if you know so much, why didn't you call her yourself*. To keep the peace, she pressed her lips together and said nothing.

Louise added, "If she isn't there, Barbara might know where she is." Conversation slid on to Louise's daughter's latest courtroom achievements.

That night Mary relayed to Ed the speculation posited by Louise that Beryl might be staying with a friend on Sycamore Street. "Do you know Barbara Fletcher?"

"Nope. Never heard the name. Stop worrying. Matt and Jason said she wasn't home, so as far as I'm concerned, that's the end of it. She's not our responsibility." He turned back to the news program on tv.

After Mary got ready for bed that night, she plucked the village phone book from under her nightstand and thumbed through for Barbara Fletcher's number. B. Fletcher was listed, and she considered calling, but it was almost 10 o'clock, a bit late to call a stranger, so decided against it, thinking she would call in the morning. When saying her prayers, she added, "Please watch over Beryl, wherever she is, and may she be home safe and sound." Relieved of her burden, she smiled, climbed into bed, and turned her attention to the book club she was hosting the following evening. She decided white chili was the perfect dish to serve since spring was not quite there yet.

That week the snow began its slow goodbye. Porches began

to reappear. Through the wind and snow that shoulder season, Matt occasionally thought of the old lady and wondered how she could live like that. He had passed Jason on the street and inquired if he'd seen her, and Jason shrugged. "I saw footprints to and from the side porch, so she must be around. I cleared a path to the house for her. Don't worry about the rumors. People like a mystery, especially close to home. It makes them feel more alive."

That same day the police department received a call from a relative of Mrs. Beryl Grant, who lived at 12 Maple Street, stating that she had not been heard from and would they check on her. Officer Josh Rudansky was dispatched to investigate, along with Matt and Rob Miller, another volunteer from the fire department. They received no response and broke down the door. Stepping over a sprawling pile of mail and newspapers, the officer directed the firemen to search the back while he headed to the front.

Matt, in the lead, soon stood in a narrow walkway that sliced through mounds of garbage bags and newspapers up to his shoulders that he'd seen prior. He whistled one low note. "Just the weight of this must have weakened the joists. Let's make this quick."

Rob whistled long and low, staring in disbelief.

Matt's limbs tingled with adrenaline. This was the most excitement he'd had since the police raid on the meth lab at the edge of town. He was there with a fire truck in case of an explosion.

On the ground floor of Beryl's house, they found a dingy bathroom with a claw-foot tub full of empty tin cans and jars. Furniture stacked haphazardly hindered passage in an adjoining room. Negotiating the obstacle course, Matt shoved a table with two chairs atop out of the way and proceeded to what he surmised was at one time the back entrance to the house.

Large garden implements leaned against a wall beside a step ladder. A hand saw, pruning shears, and an ax sprawled on the floor in front of a wooden crate spilling small hand tools.

Matt wondered why the woman didn't keep them outside on a porch, which he presumed was beyond the back door. Rob pulled on the doorknob, but it wouldn't budge.

"Let me try." Matt stepped to the door.

"Be my guest."

It yielded to Matt's weight. Immediately, they were assaulted with the putrid smell of decay. Matt's face collapsed. He locked eyes with Rob, who covered his nose.

Matt's rescue training revved into high gear as he prepared for the worst scenario. Without warning, chitters and scrabbles of claws exploded, and flashes of black and gray raced out of sight. "What the hell?"

Rob's' voice quivered in the aftermath of the varmints' escape. "I think it was raccoons."

Natural light from overhead streaked through evergreen branches attached to a living hemlock tree that stretched through the roof, long ago having forced it to give way. Broken plywood, insulation, and shingles cascaded. The floor was partially rotted away, making it treacherous to go further. Every step could cause a fall to whatever lay below. Rob looked around, his mouth unhinged like a trap door.

Matt shone a flashlight into shadowed corners and saw what appeared to be the rotting corpse of a raccoon on top of a green garbage bag, one of many that were ripped open, their contents scattered across the floor. "Now we know where she puts her garbage."

Rob sighed with relief. "Thank god it's only a raccoon." They retreated inside the house, slamming the door behind them.

Cardboard boxes filled with miscellaneous kitchen appliances, magazines, and newspapers blocked two sides of an olive-green refrigerator and saw scant provisions, nothin past its sell-by date. This indicated to the officer the occupant had prepared for a lengthy time away.

Beyond the kitchen, he spied the front room. Relief poured

through him like a shot of whiskey as he stepped in. A glance revealed a library chock full of books and magazines perched on shelves made of two-by-fours and cement blocks. They covered every wall, including the front door. Stacks of old newspapers and magazines had invaded this room as well, climbing up and over everything in their way.

In the center back wall, a fireplace with a screen interrupted encroaching stacks. Charred remains of corrugated cardboard lay in the grate. A threadbare easy chair was the only piece of furniture. On the seat was a book *Birds of The Eastern United States*. Studying the nearest shelf of books, he observed many about natural history, the environment, and global warming. He wondered, was she an environmentalist gone off the deep end?

Hurrying to a stairway leading to the basement, he descended slowly, testing each step to determine it could support his weight. Wood crackled underfoot. He noted a partial dirt floor toward the back, common in 19th-century houses in town. Sweeping the area with his flashlight, warren-like spaces ran in all directions. One led to an old furnace and water heater. Rodent droppings were sure signs mice were snugly ensconced inside for the winter. Overhead, pipes presented a hazard to any adult of average height. Thick cobwebs hung from them like remnants of ghosts. Bending his tall frame, he threaded between debris to the front, where a door gaped open. He surmised it probably led to an old storage room. As he approached, an unpleasant odor of decay permeated the air.

Upstairs, Matt and Rob had stopped at the top of the basement stairs. Matt shouted, "Josh? Are you down there?"

"Yes. I found her. Don't come down!"

The color drained from Matt's face and his body flushed with a momentary weakness. Gaining control after several seconds, he leaned his back against a wall and waited. Rob stood across from him, eyes flitting across the hazardous interior. Neither spoke.

The officer found Beryl under a heavy, metal shelving unit

in a room used as a pantry. Broken glass jars of jam, tomato sauce, and assorted preserved vegetables and fruit splattered the body and surrounding floor. He deduced that when the woman attempted to remove something from a high shelf, the unit became unstable, fell over, and crushed her. A jolt like electricity surged through him. A strong odor of vinegar emanated from a broken jar of cucumbers strewn just inches beyond her grasp. The outstretched arm indicated she must have attempted to reach one before succumbing to her injuries. She appeared to have been alive for a period of time "My God," he whispered.

He ascended the stairs to talk to the firemen. Without disclosing details, he said she was dead. It looks like an accident, but in opinion, she lived for some time after."

Matt swallowed hard and shook his head in disbelief. "Damn! Any idea how long?"

Without answering, the officer fished a phone from his pocket and called for a forensic team.

"Can you tell when she died?" Matt couldn't hide the quiver in his voice.

"No. I've seen a person live three days without food or water. I'll have to wait for the coroner's report. It's a damn shame."

Word spread through the neighborhood like virulent flu. Later that afternoon, Anne and Gail, along with other neighbors, spilled onto porches and solemnly watched as the covered remains of Beryl were placed in an ambulance. As it pulled away, they averted their eyes from one another and scuttled back inside.

Anne scoured newspapers for information on Beryl's death. She had not sought to speak to anyone on the street since Beryl's body was discovered. The neighbors learned she had been alive the day after the St. Patrick's Day party. When neighbors passed one another, they simply exchanged greetings and hurried on as if they had an appointment.

Anne remarked to Gail that the atmosphere had changed in the neighborhood.

Gail set her mug of coffee on the counter and said kindly,

"I think you're letting your imagination run away with you. The wind is too fierce to stay out long this time of year. Things will return to normal come April; you'll see." An obituary appeared in The Sentinel. Anne learned Beryl was 62, had five children, and her husband had predeceased her.

Anne shook her head. "What a shame the funeral will be private."

"We shouldn't be surprised."

Anne closed the paper and sighed. "Even though Beryl lived in that house 25 years, no one will have a chance to pay their respects."

Caught in the Undertow

Jodie lay in bed, hands over ears, pretending shouts from her parents' room were waves rushing to shore and rolling away. A breeze expanded lace curtains at the window, a white sail on the horizon. *Bang!* At the slamming of the bedroom, she jumped. The house shuddered. Heavy footsteps passed her room without pausing, were softened by the braided rug in the living room, grew louder again across the foyer to the front door, familiar *umpff* when the front door was tugged open. She waited for the second slam, but an uneasy silence held her breath in its palm. She visualized her father's mitt-size hand resting on the brass doorknob. The door closed not with a bang, but a dull thud, the anger squeezed out of it. She lay still, ears on heightened alert. The dizzy buzz of a trapped fly and a chorus of crickets from the back yard threatened to drown the sounds she strained to hear. The car door closed once, no, twice.

In the distance a dog barked a series of short, deep-throated sounds, maybe warning that someone had entered its territory. The car engine hummed to life and a few seconds later her father, Earl Taylor, screeched up the hill. Jodie listened to the car fade away into the night beyond Stanton Road, speeding toward the city where her mother said he went.

In the terrible silence, Jodie felt her body tilt toward the edge of a precipice as an inexplicable longing leapt from every pore. Countless nights after, she replayed those minutes over in her mind. He had not given her a thought, considered what she might feel, as if she mattered less than his stuff he left behind.

He would at least probably come back the next weekend to get *that*.

It seemed to Jodie she had spent her whole life separating from people and places she loved. First was her best childhood friend, Shirley. One night at supper, when she was eight, her dad had announced, "We're moving to Maryland, just outside our nation's capital," like it was paradise, a dreamy smile playing around his lips. She had lived on the farm her whole life and didn't want to leave. When she said goodbye to Shirley, Jodie waved and cried until her friend disappeared from sight.

Granny Bryce, in a nursing home in the nearest town, was her only grandparent still alive. The family visited her the weekend before they moved. Jodie had clung to her neck and sobbed until her mom pulled her gently loose and held her hand as they walked away. Granny died shortly after. Jodie was convinced she died of a broken heart.

Then a year ago, when she was thirteen, her brother, Curtis, enlisted in the army and was sent to Iraq in as part of Operation Inherent Resolve. That's what he told Mom before he left the U.S.

June unraveled into summer vacation from school. In mid-July, Jodie's dad called to invite her and a friend to see *Hamlet* at Wolf Trap Theater, an outside stage in Virginia. A Shakespeare production was not a theatrical experience she was excited about, but her mother said she should go since he was making the effort to see her.

When he arrived on the appointed evening, Jodie was dismayed to see another woman usurping her mother's place in the front seat beside him. Her name was Connie, short for Consuela. Jodie swallowed her anger, gritted her teeth, grateful her closest friend, Linda, was along for the show. Jodie responded to the woman's heavily accented questions with clipped answers, digging her nails into the car upholstery.

During intermission, she and Linda escaped to the concession stand. Her dad passed her ten dollars to paid for drinks and they wandered to the food truck parked a considerable distance from the stage.

"Did you see Dad's date flirted with him? I can't believe he brought her. It makes me sick!" She clamped her quivering bottom lip with her front teeth, her face flushing a deep pink.

Linda, the voice of reason, tried to calm her down. "I know it's awful, but you'll get through it. Just try not to say anything you'll regret, okay?"

Jodie nodded and took a few gulps of cola. An announcement from a loudspeaker drew them back to the theater and they threaded their way through the crowd to their seats.

The first line of Hamlet's famous soliloquy was seared into Jodie's mind in a slight Spanish accent, which she would have liked had the woman not been batting her eyes at her dad.

On the way home Jodie answered questions from her father, in an abrupt way that she hoped would convey she was angry with him.

Linda was dropped at home on the parallel street. When they pulled up to the curb to deliver Jodie, she managed a curt, "Thanks. Good night," slammed the door, and stalked inside without looking back. She was shaking when she got inside. Kicking off her shoes, she plunked down next to her mom, Fran. Seeing Jodie's dark mood, she puckered her lips in concern over her daughter. "I take it you didn't have a good time?"

"It was totally boring," replied Jodie, not wishing to upset her mother by telling her about the girlfriend.

They fell silent when the latest news came on. After Curtis was shipped to Iraq they had begun listening for locations of battles and pored over a map to pinpoint where it was exactly. Curtis hadn't contacted them in a long time, but finding where he might be made them feel more connected to him, in case particular places were mentioned in the newscasts. She wondered what he would say if he knew about dad's girlfriend.

The following morning, Jodie awoke early with powerful menstrual cramps and trudged to the kitchen as her mom was getting ready for work. "Good morning. I'm almost out of period pads. Can you buy some on your way home tonight?" she asked, as she reached for the Midol. It was strange how with Curtis gone, she could run around in her baby doll pajamas and speak openly about her period, she would gladly trade this freedom for his insults and surly attitude, if he would come home safe.

That afternoon, she went to Linda's to sunbathe in the back yard. Jodie imagined the day when she wouldn't need a padded bikini top to look like she had breasts. At fourteen, she figured she would have them by now, but they stubbornly refused to grow beyond size 32A. Lying in the burning sun, the previous evening's intrusion by the woman rekindled the anger, which rose to boiling point. Linda spiraled up the volume on WPGC, the local rock station, so they could time their sunbathing to its jingle: "Time to turn, so you won't burn."

Without warning, a man appeared in a yard kitty-cornered to Linda's, his face red and distorted. "Would you kids have a little consideration for someone else and turn that racket down? I can't hear myself think!" Linda immediately lowered the volume so they could barely hear it themselves. When the neighbor left, they looked at each other, mouths open in surprise. Jodie's face stung with embarrassment and slid sideways into rage. "How dare he yell at us! If he'd asked us nicely, we would have turned it down. I'd like to just…" the sentence hung in the air like a disturbed wasp while she fumed. A plan formed in her mind as she slathered more sun lotion onto her fair skin, glancing with envy at Linda's golden tan.

Mid-afternoon Linda's mom called her inside to get dressed. They were going shoe shopping for school. The two friends made a pact to meet at the top of Stanton Road at one a.m.

After work, Fran arrived with dinner from MacDonald's, which they ate at the kitchen dinette while they chatted about their day. Fran said, "You look like you got a lot of sun. You'd better put something on it before you go to bed. I think there's some Noxzema in the medicine cabinet."

After watching Jay Leno together, they went to bed. Even

though the one air conditioner, in her mom's bedroom, pushed cool air in her direction, it dissipated before reaching her. The heat was oppressive. Long ago Jodie had given up wishing for air conditioning. She kept flipping her pillow to the cool side, waiting for her mother to go to sleep so she could sneak out to meet Linda. Unable to get cool, she slid up from the damp sheet and stepped into the hall. Her mom left her door open so cooler air circulated. Jodie tiptoed to the open door of her mom's bedroom.

Jodie nipped into the bathroom for a Dixie cup of water, just in case her mom somehow sensed her plan to go out. Sometimes her mom could just tell if she was up to something. Way back in elementary school, her mother had whispered she had a gift of a sixth sense, a secret Jodie had tucked away.

"Good-night, Hon. I love you."

Her mom said that a lot since her dad left.

"Love you too," she responded, getting teary-eyed. Her thoughts jumped around like popcorn popping. She wondered if her mom missed her dad, or was glad she didn't have to argue anymore.

In the sticky heat Jodie was too hot and decided to lay on the living room couch, which at least had air circulating from mom's bedroom. Slipping into the kitchen, she poured herself a glass of water from the jug stored in the refrigerator. Condensation dripped down the glass and she placed it against her cheek, the cold a balm to her thirsty skin. She opened the door to the pantry to smell the scents of clove, cinnamon, and ginger that hung in the air. The aromas hinted of faraway places she intended to visit one day: Marrakesh, Timbuktu, Katmandu. She loved the way they felt in her mouth, rolled over her tongue like a wish.

The cat clock over the kitchen table ensured time was passing, its tail tick, tick, ticking away minutes. Returning to her room, here mom softly whistled in sleep.

Jodie dressed in a halter top and shorts. As she eased out the back door humid night air dropped on her like a cloak. The moon was creamy and luminous. Looking up, she aligned her thumb and forefinger on either side, pretended to pluck the pearl from the recesses of its darkness, and pressed it against her throat where a necklace might hang.

The asphalt of Stanton Road shimmered like a deep purple river and her bare feet slapped freely as she padded up the hill. Linda was already there, floating in a pool of light. Her hair swirled around her shoulders in damp, dark tendrils. When she saw Jodie, she lifted a toilet paper roll in one hand, and made a victory sign with the other. Jodie waved back with a roll of her own. They giggled and swam through the thick heat, like giddy mermaids gone mad.

Light and shadow splashed on well-tended front yards. The girls went straight to the house of the man who had yelled at them that day and dived into darkness, draping toilet paper on shoulders of trees, wrapping bushes like Christmas garlands, taking time to admire their artistry. Loosely twirled streamers attached hydrangea bushes to porch rails. Jodie tied a strand to a weeping cherry tree and looped the other end to the bumper of a car as if it were about to pull it out by its roots and tow it away.

When they were satisfied with the decorations, they waded down the street, keeping to the shadows as much as possible. To throw off suspicion of Linda's neighbor, they wrapped another yard across the street whose occupants were unknown. Afterwards, they steered clear of the Phillips' house, rumored to be haunted. The unkempt yard, cracked driveway scored with weeds, a crepe myrtle pushed against one side of the house where mortar between bricks was crumbling. Jodie whispered to Linda that Mother Nature had taken possession. Branches and small limbs from recent thunderstorms clung to shingles and gutters. The thought occurred to Jodie that if the house were a person, it had died and was being sealed inside a weird coffin.

Linda whispered, "It gives me the creeps to know Billy's room is just like it was when he left for Afghanistan."

Jodie pointed at the rocking chair on the front porch.

"Remember how he sat out there and read all those books for college? I heard that some nights it rocks all by itself when there isn't a breath of a breeze."

Linda added, "I heard a light bulb shines from the bathroom where his mother, you know, did it."

Jodie looked at the windows which corresponded to those in her own house and shivered. "Let's get out of here."

Paper was left on Jodie's toilet roll, and she tugged on Linda's arm. "Come on. I have an idea!" They ran towards the bottom of the street where it intersected with a wider thoroughfare. A park lay at the far side with no houses adjacent. An eerie mist rose from the creek winding through the park. The place smelled earthy, damp, full of secret living things.

Jodie tied the end of the toilet roll to a stop sign at the intersection and unrolled it across the street, securing the other end to a telephone pole. She grinned at Linda, who was laughing so hard she clamped her hand over her mouth as a muffler. At the sound of a car approaching, they ducked behind a clump of lush, overgrown bushes several yards from the road. First, loud rumbling. Headlights splayed across the road as it crested the hill. Jodie peeked around the bush just as the car broke through the paper barrier. Glee changed to horror as the driver slammed on the brakes and the car careened sideways on two wheels, screeching to a halt facing the opposite direction, parallel to their hiding place.

Two men leaped from the vehicle. Through spaces in the bushes Jodie saw one under the streetlight wearing a t-shirt which showed off muscular biceps. He shouted obscenities as he rushed to see what they had hit. He examined the ripped paper. She shrank into the bush.

"What the devil was that?" a slurred voice came from the man further away. "It looked like a board across the road."

The closer one cursed in a deep voice, "Damn! No harm done."

Jodie trembled and bit her lower lip. Her heart slammed

against her chest. She tried to disappear, heedless of branches scratching face and body. Jodie flinched as Linda dug nails into her arm. Her pulse thrummed in her ears like a distant drum. Her nostrils flared with the smell of the man as he approached their hiding place. She took tiny breaths and willed herself not to move a muscle.

After a silence that seemed to last forever, the man said, "It's only toilet paper! Probably just a prank by some dumb ass kids. Looks like they're long gone. Too bad. I'd like to teach them a lesson if they were here." The sound of a fist slamming into an open palm was unmistakable.

The voice faded. "Come on, man; I'm thirsty. Let's go." Footsteps receded toward the car. Two doors slammed and the engine growled and sped away.

After the sound died away, the girls kept still to make sure it wasn't a trick to lure them out of hiding. Once convinced, they staggered from the shadows, still shaking, and ran all the way to Jodie's house. Safely in her yard, Jodie carefully lifted the metal latch on the back gate. She mouthed and pointed to a raised sash above the patio," *Shhhh*, My mother." They sneaked to the farthest corner of the yard.

The land dropped steeply, which was no end of annoyance when Jodie mowed the grass, but it created a secret pocket, hidden from view of the house. Chain link fences spliced the land in all directions, creating boundaries and obstacles that glowed silver in the moonlight.

Out of sight from her house, they collapsed onto the ground and dissected what had happened and what could have happened. Exhilaration of secret revenge and narrow escape exploded into laughter. Washing over Jodie in waves, she laughed until her sides ached. Tears sprang to her eyes and she began to relax until she saw Linda pounding the ground, head thrown back in the throes of unfettered glee.

Finally, calm seeped into Jodie's body, flushed her limbs. Her fear and anger leaked onto the grass to mingle with falling dew. The warm breath of the earth against her cheek held the scent of summer. In the ensuing quiet, she lay drenched in moonlight. She thought of all that had happened since the disastrous night with her dad. Her mind drifted among the stars, and she knew even though her world had changed, she was going to be all right.

Sticks and Stones

Peter kicked the front door open and stormed out of the house into the web of pedestrians on Blarney Street. Though it was evening, the sun was still high, and so warm the tarmac shifted under his feet as he crossed to the shady side. Eight steely notes clanged from St. Anne's church tower and lingered sluggishly above the simmering River Lee, which wound around Cork like a noose.

He swung his burley in the air, as if carving a path through which he could pass and headed for the shop to kill time before meeting the lads. Inside O'Shea's the temperature was deliciously cool, and he breathed in the sweet odor of overripe apples and fresh pastries. Determined to bury the argument with his parents, he sidled down the nearest aisle to the magazines. A *Spiderman* comic seemed to call out, familiar as a chum. He fingered the cover, eagerly flipped through, until Mrs. O'Shea's grating bawl dragged him from the fantasy world.

"This isn't a library. Buy something or move on."

"Bloody hell," he muttered under his breath. He flung the comic onto the adjoining shelf, disturbing a delicately balanced card display, which scattered to the floor.

She rushed over roaring, "You blackguard! You've no respect for anything. I don't want you in here again. I know who you are. You're barred; do you hear me? Barred!"

He shrugged and brushed past her. Pretending to fall against the sweet display, he palmed two Lion bars, stuffed them in his pocket as he tore back into the heat.

He had dreamed thirteen would be different, that being a teen meant new privileges, freedom to stay out late, do exciting things with older lads at night, a new start. His imaginings had not framed anything specific, just vague ideas, but it had turned out to be a big disappointment; just like the whole summer, my whole stinking life, he fumed. With the curved tip of the hurley he smacked the hard ground beside the foot path, scooped a shallow grave for the empty Club Orange bottle abandoned there.

It's not my fault I've no money, he reasoned. What do they expect? The image of his burly dad forced its way into his mind: creased hands stained boot black. His ma referred to him as her St. Bernard, not simply because of his large build, but because he was kind and generous, she said he was "always eager to rescue any person or creature in distress."

When Peter was younger, he had been thrilled to go to work with him. To step into the dark little shop, the earthy smell of leather mixed with tangy polish and oil, was enticing. Everything he saw, did, was new and exhilarating. To watch his da skillfully replace a sole on a delicate high heel, the way he'd slice the leather into graceful curves and mold it, like an artist, flooded him with wonder. When the repair was complete, he allowed Peter to apply polish to the shoes, and with a soft cloth, he taught him to rub them until they shone like new. How many times had his da said with pride, "Now, that's the way a shoe should look. 'Tis grand people don't take better care of their shoes; for if they did, I'd be out of business." That was followed by a loud belly laugh.

As Peter wound up the hill, he chastised himself. What was the big deal? He just repairs peoples' stinking old shoes. You'd have to murder me before I'd do that trade. He bit into one of the chocolate bars, let the stolen sweetness melt on his tongue. A familiar voice saluted him as he trudged along.

"Hey, boyo!" His pal, Martin, crossed the street, zigzagging through traffic to catch up. He frowned as he fell in step beside Peter. "You look in foul humor. What's wrong wit' ya?"

Peter kicked a stone and words tumbled out about the row with his parents over him nicking ten euro from the kitchen counter. "You'd think I robbed the fuckin' Bank of Ireland the way they was goin' on about it. The old man says I'm useless." He mimicked his father's voice. "'You keep this up you'll turn into a right gurrier. You'll end up like your man doing time in Limerick for stealing cars if you don't cop on.' Ma isn't much better, nagging 'You used to be such a good lad. What's happened to you?' I couldn't get out o' there fast enough."

Martin sympathized, "The old ones haven't a clue, sure. They're all the same."

The boys coiled up the hill through the narrow streets. As they plodded along the footpath beside a chain of squatting houses, a Jack Russell terrier charged at them from behind a garden gate. Its small snout poked through the bars, and as Peter passed, it snapped at his ankle. He instinctively hopped away and sputtered, "That bloody dog tried to eat me leg!"

Martin sniggered, but they were nearing the empty lot where their two pals were engaged in a hurling skirmish, battling over a bare patch of earth, and they ran to join them. The latecomers teamed up against the other two and a fierce match ensued. The rare times Peter gained possession of the sliotar, balanced it on the hurley, and prepared to slam it through the imaginary goal posts, one of the opposing boys knocked into him, or by superior skill, managed to steal it and charge off in the opposite direction. Sam and Liam were trouncing them.

Up and down the field they battled. Peter chased the sliotar and slashed at it with all his might. Sweat soaked his t-shirt. He whirled around as Sam barreled towards him and was momentarily blinded by low rays of the sun. A sharp pain shot through his shoulder and travelled down his arm, the result of a blow from Sam's hurley.

"You bloody eejit! If that'd been me head, you'd have murdered me!" He slammed his stick onto the ground. "Fuck it! I'm gasping. Anybody got anything to drink?"

The boys knotted under a scraggly beech tree at the back of

the lot. Peter wriggled out of his shirt and checked his shoulder where a red welt began to appear. Tucking the shirt into the waist of his jeans, he waited as Liam rifled through a backpack and retrieved a two-liter Cola bottle filled with tap water. Peter was handed the bottle, and wiped the mouth of it on his shirt before bringing it to his lips. He was so parched, he gulped huge mouthfuls. Sam kicked him in the calf, almost sending him sprawling.

"Don't drink it all, ya greedy bastard."

"Fuck off!" Peter shouted. He had a sudden urge to pour the water over his head, but resisted, and passed it on. They collapsed against an adjacent stone wall and killed time throwing stones at crows attempting to land in the tree.

The burning midsummer sun dipped behind the western hills, sending bloody shards across the sky. The Shandon bells rang ten times, each sonorous note dragging Peter back to his days as an altar boy. He had liked the feeling of being part of something special. It had lent him a sense of belonging outside of his family. He remembered helping the monsignor with the thurible during high mass, the smoke and spicy smoke deliciously intoxicating. Another memory flashed of the priests he had known all his life, especially Father Donnelly. He was the only one who really had talked to him. He told Peter that every morning and evening the priests prayed for the people who lived on the north side of the city. A lot of good their prayers did me, he thought. I've no money, no new runners, nothing. What have all their prayers ever done for me? He gritted his teeth making the facial muscle over his jawbone pulse like a spider.

His thoughts jumped to Mrs. O'Shea barring him from the shop. His ma often sent him there to buy an item she needed. How was he going to explain he couldn't do that anymore? He felt like yelling, or hitting something or someone, preferably Sam, but knew he'd never get away with it. Sam was bigger and like a bull when he was pissed off.

Later, when he thought about what happened next, he wasn't

sure who suggested it. He only knew that after dark they all became of one mind. Sam grabbed his hurley and headed to the footpath along the crest of the hill, wielding his stick like a weapon. Liam followed, and like a game of Simon Says, copied what Sam did. Next came Martin. Peter attached to the end like the tail of a snake.

Up they clambered onto garden walls. They whacked shrubs and trees. Green confetti fluttered to the ground with every slice. Each new act made them bolder, more daring. A feverish excitement rushed through Peter. His limbs started to tingle. His mind was buzzing and yet acutely focused at the same time.

Heads of adults floated in lighted windows. A man shouted, "Stop blackguarding or I'll ring the guards. I'm warning ye."

"I'll ring the guards. I'm warning ye," Sam parroted, then exploded with sinister laughter. Looking at the window, as if daring the man to say something else, he picked up a potted plant from a stoop and smashed it on the concrete.

Peter followed the others onto the roof of a garden shed. He leapt down and with all his strength struck a trash bin. Its contents spewed across the lane. The satisfaction of destruction swelled his chest and he howled with delight, then spun around to see if any grownup dared confront him, but faces were veiled behind curtains. They rounded the corner and marched along the block below the empty lot where they had played their match earlier.

Again the terrier came at them barking. Sam jumped onto the low stone wall and opened the gate, chortling as the dog snarled and snapped at Peter's heels. Instinctively, Peter kicked it, hard. It yelped and flipped over on the cement path, then lay against the wall, sides heaving. He bent down to stare the dog in the eye. "Ya want a piece o' me? Come and get me, ya fuckin' little devil." The dog bared his teeth and growled behind quivering lips, but didn't move or even lift his head. His eye stared into Peter's, held it, waited.

Melding, menacing, moving as one hungry beast, the boys

closed in. The four formed a semi-circle, trapping the dog against the wall. Peter's pulse rushed in his ears. He held his breath until he felt he would faint. Sweat trickled into his eyes. His underarms stung with the prick of tiny needles. For one long moment he crouched, hurley in hand, eyes locked with the dog's.

The next instant he unleashed a savage fury and slammed the stick onto the dog's skull. The creature made a high squealing noise on impact, then lay still. The other lads erupted. Each struck it with his hurley. Peter hit it again, still unleashing his anger. Its body went limp, but its legs jerked with each thud. Thick streams of blood oozed from its mouth and nose.

Panting, Peter leaned on his knees. His shoulders heaved as he gulped the sweaty night air. Foul odors of wet fur and exposed body tissue assaulted his nostrils. When he dared look around, he seemed flanked by three strangers. Gradually, he became aware of the stick in his hand, stared at it like something foreign. His eyes returned to the dog. Its lifeless, mutilated body held his spent rage like a cup. He was hit simultaneously by comprehension and revulsion. His fist opened and the hurley clattered onto the footpath, but he didn't notice as he backed away into the shadows and fled towards home. Halfway there he realized his hands were empty. He had left the incriminating hurley at the scene, *C. O'Callaghan* written on it in black marker. Da will murder me if he finds out what I done. Maybe I will end up in Limerick jail.

He sneaked up the street and rounded the corner towards the crime scene. In the darkness he glided undetected, staying in the shadows away from the few working street lights. He was in front of the house next to where the dog was before he saw the outside light on and recognized the stooped figure of Mrs. Murphy, a friend of his granny. He dived onto the pavement against the wall, hoping she hadn't seen him.

Was it her dog? His hand clamped his mouth to muffle the sound trying to escape. If he'd had his hurley, he could have reached out and touched her with it. She hobbled away from the street towards her door. A pale dressing gown swallowed her withered frame and the limp body of the dog lay against her chest, cradled like a baby. He could hear her anguished sounds.

She sobbed and cried aloud, "Why? My poor darlin'. What have they done to you?"

A weight descended upon Peter so immense that momentarily he could not lift his body off the ground. Tears dashed against his eyelids, but he swallowed hard, forced them back down. He'd learned to do that when only seven years of age. Being called Nancy boy and getting beat up by older lads in the neighborhood when he showed any weakness had taught him boys aren't supposed to cry.

When the door closed behind Mrs. Murphy, he found the stick atop the storm drain in the street. As his fingers closed around it, he sighed with shaky relief. But it felt different in his hand, unpleasant, no longer a plaything. Scrambling to his feet he hurried down the hill.

At home, the family seemed to crush in on him. Instead of a place of safety, it was full of danger where he must sneak, scurry, hide. He rushed to the bathroom. Grabbing the soap he lathered, washed his face and hands. Still the sickening smell clung to him. He reached inside the tub for the towel bar and snatched a face cloth. Smearing it with soap he scrubbed and scrubbed again. He stared into the mirror. Hollow eyes accused him.

Next, he tackled the hurley. A dark stain had soaked into the porous ash. Clumps of brown and white hair stuck at the drain and he swished the bloody water around to force it down.

He opened the door, turned the light off, and listened while peeking around the frame. His brothers were watching television with his parents, sister nowhere in sight, enabling him to slip into the bedroom and stash the stick in the closet under last year's school books. He removed his shoes to get ready for bed when he noticed red splatters on them. He whipped off his jeans. Traces of similar matter flecked the frayed hem. He shoved them under the bed, tugged on a dirty pair of trousers from the closet floor, and scurried back to the bathroom with the shoes at his sides in case of an encounter. Cleaning off the blood made him gag. He flushed the toilet to mask the sound, and wiped them as best he could, hoping it was enough. Slipping back to his room, he lay in the dark, reliving the events from the beginning.

If only Sam hadn't opened the gate. If only we hadn't gone up that street. If only I'd kept walking. He couldn't get the sound out of his head, the dull *thunk!* of the hurley against the furry body. He thrashed from side to side. When his brothers turned in for the night, he pretended to be asleep. He tossed and trembled, dropping into a fitful sleep near dawn. When he awoke, after five carefree seconds, the image of Mrs. Murphy cuddling the dog slammed into his brain. Her words clawed at his conscience.

He stayed in bed listening for routine sounds of his da leaving the house. When he heard the front door close, he eased from bed and slunk into the kitchen where his ma sat at the table with a mug of coffee reading *The Examiner*. She glanced over the top and seeing Peter, set it down.

"You're up early. Not sick, are you?"

"Not great. I think I'm just hungry." He retrieved the milk from the refrigerator, pulled a box of Frosties from the cupboard, and poured a bowlful.

His mother said, "I hope you're not getting a bug. This warm weather is a breeding ground for 'em. Maybe it's just a guilty conscience." She picked at a glob of dried strawberry jam beside her mug on the oilcloth.

The color drained from his face, and he lowered his spoon. How could she know? He stammered, "What are you on about?"

She wiped the finger, sticky with jam, on her apron. "If you've forgot what you did, then you don't understand how dreadful 'tis to rob your own. How do you expect us to trust you now?"

Without answering, Peter managed to swallow a few bites when a knot in his stomach warned him to stop. His ma, having observed his first mouthful, thus establishing health, assumed the discussion was over and returned to the paper.

A weary sigh escaped her lips. "The devil lives in temptation. It only takes getting caught on the street once and word spreads like the plague. Remember what your da says: Your reputation is like a pair of shoes. It goes everywhere with you."

Trying to compose his erratic thoughts, Peter said, "I'll go to confession on Saturday if 'twill make you happy. It's the only time I ever done it." Unbidden, the chocolate bars he'd nicked from O'Shea's shot into his mind. *Am I like that?* On his way out, he turned and said softly, "Ma, I'm sorry."

She sighed and slowly shook her head.

He didn't venture out all morning, but wallowed on the sofa watching television, and tried not to think. His next younger brother, Collin, rushed in the front door at lunchtime. "Peter, you'll never guess what happened to Ma Murphy's dog!" He was bursting to deliver the grizzly news.

Peter bolted upright. "What?" He glanced toward the kitchen but steadied himself when he remembered his mother was at the hairdresser's.

Collin's eyes shone as he blurted out the details of local gossip. "Somebody killed it! Must have knocked it down and run over it. 'Twas flat as a pancake! They dumped it outside her gate. That's what some of the lads say."

"What lads?" Peter demanded.

"Sam Ryan and Jimmy B. But some people up there say they thought 'twas some hooligans late last night. Said they was trashin' the place 'round about ten o'clock. Sure, weren't you up there last night?"

"No! I hung out at Martin's place last night. Why? Did they say I was there?" A cold shiver crawled up his spine.

"No. I just thought you was there is all. You're always up

there playin' hurley, sure."

"Well, I wasn't there."

Collin added, "I remember seeing you come in when we were watching the film last night. You went straight to our room, quiet as a ghost. You never do that." His eyes narrowed accusingly. "You were there, ya liar. You know something; I can tell."

Peter's face turned red and he shouted. "Bloody hell! I tell ya I wasn't there!"

Collin shrugged and loped toward the kitchen, leaving Peter to wonder whether he should find Martin and solidify an alibi. He wasn't sure he could face him or any of the lads. He collapsed back onto the sofa and pushed the remote, letting the boring afternoon programming on RTE numb his senses.

The afternoon heat, combined with the small quarters, closed in on him. He started pacing from the kitchen to the bedroom, back to the sitting room. He couldn't eat, couldn't sleep. Remorse that had seeded itself overnight grew to a tentacled vine. It was less than twenty-four hours since it happened but the tick, tick, tick of the kitchen clock made him want to jump out of his skin. He had to do something. He pounded on his temples to try and obliterate the vision of Ma Murphy holding her dead pet. A wave of certainty rolled over him. His da would surely find out what he had done. There was only one thing to do.

He pushed into the bustle of the city, turned south toward the river. Lost and alone in anguish, it was as if he were outside his own body. His arms and legs moved independently from his control. At the corner, he paused, and his eyes raked the familiar quayside rooftops below, his da's shop, the crooked line continuing to his best pal Martin's Street two blocks beyond. The clamor of church bells swooped around him like a flock of crows. A glare of sunlight reflecting off the river left him disoriented, light-headed. Drawn by a powerful impulse, he let it lead him. Surrender was as natural as rain.

Lilies in the Field

Rain was falling hard as the fisherman headed for the shelter of a clump of trees down river. A thick growth of brush and overhanging limbs closed over him like an umbrella, and he slid off his hood. As he leaned down to place his fishing gear under a tangle of bushes, his hand brushed against something out of place. He moved aside woven branches to get a better look.

At his feet lay a burlap bundle. He tugged the package from its bower for a closer look. Hoping for a treasure, perhaps a cache of goods hidden by the IRA when it was active in this corner of County Cork, his fingers found a corner and flipped it back. "Holy Mother of God," he murmured. A wave of nausea swept over him as he looked at the face of a dead newborn infant. The skin was a putrid blue-gray and the tiny body was as cold and hard as limestone along the riverbank. He replaced the bundle, threw on his hood, and headed to the garda station.

Gossip slashed through the town like a razor, leaving behind shredded and bloodied reputations. People spoke in hushed tones on street corners and at front gates. Many stayed near home, trying to protect their children from knowledge of something they themselves could not understand.

In a farmhouse overlooking the River Blackwater, on the outskirts of town, Lilian O'Leary was busy preparing dinner for her family when a knock on the door caused her to jump. She cautiously peeped through the lace curtains and saw two familiar gardai.

Opening the door she said, "Hello Sergeant Flynn, Sean." She hoped her voice sounded normal.

"Hello, Mrs. O'Leary," Sergeant Flynn answered.

"Good evening, Lilian," said Sean Powers, the younger officer.

"Won't ye come in? Would ye have a cup of tea?" She showed them into a small dining area adjacent to the kitchen and offered them a seat at the table. "I've the kettle on already."

The sergeant removed his hat and studied the room. "No, thank you. We just wanted to ask you a few questions and we'll be on our way."

"Ye don't mind if I keep on with making the dinner while we talk, do ye?" she asked. "Gerard will be home in a few minutes and he likes his food on the table."

"Carry on. I can understand that," he said with a smile. "I'm a bit like that myself."

She turned quickly to the counter and resumed chopping vegetables, concealing her trembling hands.

Sergeant Flynn began, "I'm sure you know why we're here. You've heard about the baby that was found yesterday down by the river?"

"I have," she answered. "God love the poor child."

"Did you see anything suspicious down this way the last few days? Any strangers about?"

"Not at all," she said. "Haven't seen a soul."

He stood and walked to the window. "I notice from here you can almost see the bend where the baby was found.

"Have you heard of any girl in town that hasn't been seen the last few weeks? You know how word gets out about such things."

"I can't say as I can think of anyone, Sergeant, but I haven't been about the town much lately. Just nipped in to pick up a few things at Tesco." Mrs. O'Leary replied, glancing over her shoulder without turning around.

"Well, if you do recollect something, sure, you'll let us know." He stood and turned to leave.

The sergeant ran fingers through his graying hair and studied

Lilian as he turned to leave. "By the way, if you don't mind me asking, where's Lily? I understand she hasn't been in school for close to a fortnight."

Lilian turned from the counter and led the two men to the front door, avoiding eye contact. "She's been thrown down with the flu. I'm just getting over it myself. I was so sick she stayed home taking care of me for a few days. With this miserable weather it's a wonder we haven't all got pneumonia."

The sergeant replaced his hat and left, followed by Sean. "Thank you, Lilian. I hope Lily is better soon."

"Thanks very much." She closed the door and leaned her forehead against it to quell her rising fear.

When Gerard O'Leary returned home from five days on the road, he was full of questions for his wife, having heard about the abandoned baby on the car radio.

"Do they know how long it was there? Have they any leads on the whore?"

She squeezed her lips together, spooned out a steaming plateful of stew, and plunked it down in front of him. She answered quietly, "I heard 'twas a couple of days. Nobody seems to know much, but I've never heard so many rumors flying about the place. Everyone's already tried and convicted the mother before they even know what happened or who she is."

"And why wouldn't they?" Gerard wanted to know. "Tisn't something that happens in this town every day, you know; thank God for that." He crossed himself and proceeded to devour his food. "I hope 'tis not one of Lily's friends, for she'll never darken the inside of this house again. If I knew who 'twas, I'd turn her in myself, by God."

The kitchen was drowned in silence, save for the scraping and slurping of Gerard eating. With her knife Lilian pushed her food around in the gravy, making tiny dark islands with chunks of meat.

Gerard belched loudly and pushed his empty plate away. "Is Lily out of bed?"

"Not yet. She hasn't been able to keep a thing down since you left. Her fever is finally gone, so I suspect she'll be up tomorrow." Lilian rose from the table to signal what she hoped was an end to the conversation, and began to clear the debris of the meal.

On Sunday morning she was urging toast on her daughter when Gerard sauntered into the kitchen. "It's time to get ready for mass, girls. We don't want to be late. It's my turn to take the eucharist to the sick so I must be early. Chop-chop." He smacked his hands together twice.

Lily put down her toast. "Da, I really don't feel up to going."

Her father raised his voice. "If you're well enough to get out of bed, you're well enough to go to mass. Let's get going. You've been in the house what—over a week now. That's long enough to give in to anything. I've never missed a day of work in my life."

Lily looked up wearily, "I know, I know. You've told me a hundred times."

Gerard leaned over the table and whacked Lily on the head with the back of his hand. She shrieked in pain. "Don't be cheeky with me, young lady."

Lilian leapt to her daughter's defense. "For goodness' sake, Gerard, the poor child's been near death's door with the flu. Let her be."

At this, Gerard lunged at Lilian. His fingers twisted around the hair at the nape of her neck and yanked downward until her chin slanted upwards. "How dare you side with her against me, Woman. You ever do that again and you'll regret it," he snarled. "Do I have to give you another lesson on who's boss in this house? Now, hurry on, both of you," he commanded, releasing his grip.

Lilian took several deep breaths. She turned, laid her hands on Lily's shoulders and stared Gerard in the eyes. "She doesn't feel like going and neither do I. We're not going."

Gerard was stunned by her defiance, and didn't come at her again. Something in her tone, a strange glint in her eyes, kept him at bay. Cursing them both, he stalked out.

The next morning, he left for work early. As soon as Lilian heard the engine fade away, she tiptoed down the hall and stood at Lily's door, watching her sleep. Her stomach tightened in a knot as she remembered the dreadful ordeal of the week before.

Her daughter's labor had been excruciating over ten hours. "I'm glad she's dead," Lily whispered when it was all over. "I would never want her to live here with him."

What an enormous relief to Lilian that the baby came while her husband was out of town.

"I'll take her down by the river tonight," she said.

"Mam, I'm going with you," Lily stated simply.

To her mother, she looked and sounded older than she had the day before and it ripped at her heart.

"All right, pet." She stayed until Lily fell asleep.

After midnight Lilian gently awakened Lily and helped her dress. She had gingerly wrapped the child in a soft white towel and then in protective burlap.

As they slipped out the back door, she supported her daughter with one arm while clutching her grandchild to her breast, joining the three of them into one. It was for Lilian the longest journey of her life, across the hard, half-frozen stubble field to the river, cloaked in a sadness blacker than the darkness around them.

When at last they reached the stand of trees near the bend she loosened her hold on her daughter. Lily eased herself against a tree and reached for the child. As she knelt on the ground and placed her baby under a low evergreen bush, she melted into the earth and seemed a part of it.

Lilian was seized by an irrational fear that Lily was dying too. An urgency swirled through her. She could not let the night end like this, in death and silence. For several minutes they knelt there shivering, shrouded in their own thoughts and feelings.

Then Lilian slid her arm around her daughter and pulled her to her breast. She began to rock her as she had when Lily was a baby. Unaccustomed to such tenderness, Lily responded by clutching her mother and burying her face in her bosom. Her body convulsed. Tears burst forth as turbulent as the Blackwater which drowned out her keening.

Lilian held her, rocked her, cooed and comforted her, fusing their painful secret forever, until Lily had no tears left. For hours they stayed entwined, ethereal beings unaware of their surroundings, whispering to one another. When they finally rose, it was like two ghosts rising from the grave into the night, pale and fierce, and with frightening determination.

Throne of the Third Heaven

"Jubilation! Salvation! Revelation!" James, gray work shirt rolled above elbows, reaches for the brown metal trash can beneath the desk, empties it into the receptacle on the equipment cart. Propped beside the desk is an ink blotter he notices has been replaced with a new one on the desk top. He rolls up the discard, secures it with a rubber band from his shirt pocket, and places it inside a burlap sack he keeps on a hook of the cart. In the stillness a hymn bubbles up and he sings softly, "I saw the light, I saw the light..."

Gnarled, calloused fingers ease back around the smooth, wooden mop handle like an extended arm, and drive it over the floor with renewed purpose. He often thinks of people who held the mop before him, a line of folks who cleaned and polished the same three floors in the General Services Administration. Sometimes it feels like they're stubbornly hanging onto a job that continues without them, spying from the shadows, raising an eyebrow as they compare his skill to their own, and perhaps find him wanting. Methodically, he shines his way in and out of offices down the long hall. Dipping mop into bucket, twirling the strings like a dancer, gliding, sliding, mopping, stopping. Emptying trash, sometimes finding treasure he places in the sack, dipping, wringing, singing, until the night shift is over.

A silhouette leaning against the last door frame, he closes his eyes for a moment of rest. Then, stowing the cart in the utility closet, he heads to the washroom. From his pants pocket he fishes a hand brush, softens it under the hot water faucet, places it on the right-hand corner of the sink. Soothing scent of pine disinfectant soap wafts around him as he piles sluggish liquid into his palm. Memory flashes of home down south in pine tree country, and his elementary school that oozed the same smell in the classroom, and privy out back. He lathers, rubs up and over his elbows, retrieves the brush to scrub deep creases in his knuckles and under thickening nails. Fluorescent lights buzz overhead. In the mirror, he scrutinizes well-proportioned facial features, stretches his top lip under front teeth to check symmetry of the thin mustache and frowns. His skin almost matches the drab color of his work shirt. He takes particular care of his appearance. Behind round, wire-frame glasses, intense black eyes appear haunted, cheeks sunken, the slight frame shrunken so his head appears to float freely above the collar.

It causes him to cringe when he thinks of the previous evening when Miss Ophelia, his landlady, commented on him looking peaked in front of the other tenants. She tried to force her chicken and biscuits swimming in gravy on him even though he insisted he wasn't hungry. The past few days he's managed to keep down half bowls of chicken broth, a few mouthfuls of mashed potatoes and cups of warm tea. She doesn't pay him any mind, believing she knows best. She's like family, but he wishes she would quit trying to tell him what to do.

At 7:00 a.m. he punches out, pauses at the exit to massage the knot in his stomach that aches like a rotten molar. Outside, a shiver runs up his spine. It feels colder than usual for a November morning and he's happy to see the lights of the bus coming up the block, so he won't have to wait. Little bitty mercies. He smiles to himself.

On Constitution Avenue he stares out the window at the Capitol dome glowing against the twilight sky, imagines it's like a shining church in the Third Heaven. When the bus nears his street, he tugs the rope to signal his stop. The tinkle always makes him think of kid angels ringing tiny bells. Holding the hand bar to steady himself, he descends onto the sidewalk with an "Umph." A gust of wind flies down his collar, forcing him to clamp the wool coat under his chin. He wishes he had asked Miss Ophelia to sew a button on. Regret ain't good for nothin' but wastin' time. A missin' button be a sign a man be lettin' hisself go. When I get home, I'll ask her to sew it on for me.

He swishes through dry fallen leaves that scurry into shadows as he trudges to the former carriage house he rents from Mr. Wertlieb. The day he met the Washington businessman James had brought along his brother, Eugene, to vouch for him. Mr. Wertlieb had pulled up in a shiny new 1950 Ford Crestliner, the color of new dollar bills. When he stepped out, he brought the new car scent with him, a potent smell that conjured up for James the first time he ever rode in a car. He was seven years old. The car belonged to his Uncle George in Greenville. On the drive uptown his uncle talked to him about grabbing opportunities when they come along, while James inhaled the new car smell as he ran eager hands over the spotless interior.

At that meeting, Mr. Wertlieb had asked questions which James answered to the man's satisfaction, because a handshake was all he required to seal the deal. James hadn't laid eyes on him since.

Inside the carriage house, he pulls strings on two bare bulbs suspended from the ceiling. The glare illuminates intricately decorated objects that flash and sparkle as bright as the Potomac River at sunrise. He blinks while his eyes adjust, weaves his way to the back where a small electric heater waiting like a loyal hunting dog. Setting the burlap sack on the floor beside a plain, ladder-back chair, he plugs in the heater before folding onto his knees to pray. After several minutes, he clutches the wood surround that locks the remaining spiky canes of the chair seat in place, and struggles to his feet. The pain in his gut is enervating, but time, like an itch in his bones, is pushing him to finish. But what's it mean when it's finished? Will it disappear up to heaven?"

He moves stiffly, a heron wading upstream, through the tightly-packed mass of gleaming objects, a daily ritual of inspecting each piece for damage. Long ago he'd learned you never know when mice'll creep in and rip things apart. Just when you think everything is safe, you get careless and they get you. The inspection reveals no vermin intrusion since the previous day. He shuffles to the front, turns to survey his life's work. "Wings. Wings. Crowns and things."

The assembly is arranged as God directed him. The right side reflects Jesus and the New Testament; the left honors prophets of the Old Testament. Every object he meticulously had covered in silver and gold foil, with purple construction paper, the royal color a perfect background for embellishment. Electric cable, covered in gold foil, outlines an ornate offertory table. Celestial creations display unfurled wings, while others with smaller wings, high above on foiled poles, command symmetrical positions on each side. Pulpits, pedestals, altars— some infused with Bible verses—are ready for the Second Coming. Tall pieces on either side are labeled "Adam" and "Eve."

His first creation, a seven-pointed star, made while he was in the army, is prominent at the bottom of the center altar. On a raised platform, in position of highest honor, is the royal Throne, an intricately adorned, high-back chair with a rose-colored velvet cushion.

In the beginning, James had purchased basic carpenter tools: a wooden folding rule, a claw hammer, a small hand saw. Using scraps of cardboard and tape, tacks and glue, he began. Sometimes he bought small items like carpet tacks, gold foil, and construction paper. Old light bulbs and used aluminum foil were scavenged from trash at work. Soft drink bottles and jelly jars were easy to come by, saved for him by Miss Ophelia, or picked from trash cans along 7th Street.

On trash days, he scoured streets and alleys for old or broken furniture people had placed on the curb. He clapped with glee when he discovered a table or chair, because he needed so many. Twelve of each were needed just for the disciples. He dismantled and reconfigured them to specifications. One Saturday, he was wrestling a heavy table down the sidewalk, and a scruffy young man in a worn army jacket offered to give him a hand. "That's mighty kind of you."

James extended his hand. They shook hands and brief introductions were exchanged. The younger man's name was Mitchell. The two of them easily maneuvered the table to the garage where James explained matter-of-factly what he was doing. Instead of backing away like James was crazy, Mitchell's face lit up with a grin, revealing front teeth that protruded conspicuously over his bottom lip. He wagged his head back and forth in wonder. When he asked if James would mind if he watched him work, maybe even help if he needed it, James' heart leaped with joy. In his mind he shouted, Preacher! Teacher! Here is a strong young man willing to help. Hallelujah.

That summer, on early Saturday mornings when the city was still cool, James greeted Mitchell when he rapped on what he called the studio door and poked his head in. "Hey Mr. James. How you doin? What we getting' up to today?"

Sometimes they ventured to the gentrified neighborhoods on Connecticut Avenue to forage for discarded furniture. A couple of times Miss Ophelia's brother used his pickup truck to transport larger items.

James patiently showed Mitchell how to transform a scarred, disfigured and broken table into a thing of beauty. Each work was planned in minute detail. First it was drawn out on a chalkboard, like an instruction diagram. It took hours to complete a small object, such as a crown, cutting shapes from heavy cardboard, sculpting them by patiently curving—but never bending—adding other shapes in layers. Finally, gold and silver foil were added, and everything transformed from its former use into a part of the Throne, its position divinely ordered. Following God's instructions, James used his own head to manipulate the material for the crowns to the proper shape.

Usually, he bought bread, bologna, and icy bottles of Dr. Pepper from a local mom and pop shop, and he and Mitchell sprawled on wooden pallets against the back wall to eat lunch. James learned Mitchell had been subjected to the heavy hand of a stepfather when he was a boy and had left home at fifteen. He lived by his wits on the street until he decided to join the army, but was discharged early. No explanation was offered as to why, and James didn't ask. When he returned to D.C., he was back on the street. This time it didn't take him long to learn where he could get a hot meal and a clean bed at a shelter on rainy or cold nights, but mostly he slept in abandoned buildings.

He asked James, "How come you know so much about art?"

When James told him God gave him instructions, Mitchell shot a sideways glance at him. "You sayin' God come to you for real?"

"I wouldn't believe it either if it ain't happen to me. Alls I know about art is what I'm doin', which is what I'm told to do. I know it don't seem likely he would show Hisself to somebody like me, but..." James spread his arms to encompass the entire space. "All this be for the Second Coming. Why me? I don't know."

Mitchell shook his head. "*Mmh, mmh, mmh*. It sure looks like a miracle to me."

Over the next few months, the two became close. James told Mitchell he had come from Elloree, a little town in rural South Carolina. "My father was gone half the time, traveling the back roads of the county as an itinerant preacher. He sure could sing. He loved gospel music. Had a bass voice that could make a grown man cry."

Listening intently, Mitchell asked, "You still got folks down there?"

"I got two sisters livin' in the old home place."

He told Mitchell that his brother, Eugene, had left home during the Depression and moved to D.C. in search of opportunity. James followed a few years later, at age 22, and landed on Eugene's doorstep. Even though he had a small apartment, he let James stay with him. James quickly found a job as a short order cook nearby, in a diner on New York Avenue, and began paying his way. With his first paycheck, after giving half the rent to his brother, he bought a notebook to write down his thoughts at night after Eugene went out or retired to his room.

At twilight one April morning, James had awakened with a jolt from a deep sleep. The house was still. An unearthly quiet blanketed the city like deep snow. He crept to the window to breathe fresh air and calm down. Above the row houses across the street, he looked at the deep, starless void. He was startled when the heavens cracked open and a radiant figure emerged and spoke to him. Afterward he knelt and prayed fervently, speaking in tongues, until sounds of Eugene stirring drifted into his consciousness. He rose and dressed for the early shift at the Capital Diner. That night he retrieved the notebook from under the sofa cushions where he slept and wrote: "This is true that the great Moses the giver of the 10th commandment appeared in Washington, D.C., April 11, 1931."

One day Mitchell asked if James had fought in the war and James shared his story. In '42 he was drafted in the army; got stationed in Guam out in the middle of the Pacific. He was a carpenter sometimes, but mostly he was ordered to maintain and fortify the air field at the base around Agana Bay. That basically meant digging trenches, even though a lot of guys in his unit were professionals or had skilled labor jobs back home. "I knew of two teachers and one architect, but they had to dig ditches with the rest of us in the colored unit. It felt like the hottest place on earth, and it was the worst job a man could have."

He related that one blistering day when they took a break, he had sought the scant shade of a palm tree to watch a dolphin curl in and out of waves beyond the break. Without warning, one rose up out of the ocean, and shot across the water straight at him. He dropped his canteen and stared awestruck as it changed into a robed figure with a breastplate of silver and gold so bright it hurt his eyes. The face of a bearded man glowed like stars. It hovered just above the ground in front of James, who covered his head and shrank against the tree, shaking. The tropical heat hammered down and he dropped to the sand in a faint. Moments later he heard a deep voice like an echo inside his head, but he was too frightened to look up and stayed prostrate with his hands protecting his head.

"I have chosen you for a great purpose," it said.

James flung his head from side-to-side chanting, "Thisaintrealthisaintrealthisaintreal." He raised his head a few inches and opened his right eye to a slit. The figure was still suspended there, but the brightness had dimmed to a soft glow. "Tonight, you will begin to create a symbol of eternal peace. I will tell you how."

Later, James collected foil from packs of cigarettes littering the paths between the barracks, the latrine, and the beach. He borrowed glue from a buddy in administration and bartered for a box of thumb tacks. The material was then stowed in his locker. In time off he furtively rummaged through trash bins behind headquarters and found a scrap of sturdy cardboard. Over the next three days a seven-pointed star took shape, which he covered in silver foil and decorated with tacks. The sacred symbol was small enough to hide in his duffle where it remained until the end of the war.

He grinned as he told Mitchell about the day they learned the war had ended. "The whole base celebrated all night long. I never been so happy in my life."

After he was discharged, he returned to D.C. and worked as a handyman around the northeast section of the city near the rooming house where he stayed. Miss Ophelia hired him to repair and paint vacated rooms, and deducted the pay from his rent. One morning, when he slipped into the kitchen for a cup of coffee, she told him about a job opening for night janitor at the General Services Administration. He applied, was hired, and had worked there ever since.

For a while no visions disrupted his waking hours, but he remained vigilant for a sign of what he was supposed to do.

One evening, his patience paid off. Later that night he wrote in his notebook, "This is true that on October 2, 1946, the great Virgin Mary and the Star of Bethlehem appeared over the nation's capital." In her open hands was a gold and silver crown.

He waited. Several years after the apparition, while praying in his room, a shaft of sunlight squeezed through a gap in the blinds. It was the sign he was waiting for. That day God anointed him St. James, Director of Special Projects for the State of Eternity and commanded him to build the Throne of the Third Heaven of the Nations' Millennium General Assembly. James said to Mitchell, "That's when I started all this."

The second Saturday in October, Mitchell didn't show up. James figured he must be feeling poorly, maybe drank too much the night before. When he didn't come the following Saturday, James left the studio and headed home early. He stopped to ask a knot of teens at a street corner if anyone had seen Mitchell. A gangly boy with an air of self assurance said, "Mitchell who?"

James said, "Mitchell is all I know. How many can there be?"

"I don't know nobody by that name," said the young man. He turned to his friends. "Y'all know any Mitchell?" They shrugged and shook their heads. James described him, making specific reference to his army jacket, long hair and buck teeth.

The apparent leader said, "We done told you we never seen him. We don't know nobody named Mitchell. He sound like he so ugly we'd remember if we seen him." Rude laughter exploded from the boys. The leader crushed the butt of his cigarette into the sidewalk and thrust his shoulders back. "And we know everybody; ain't that right." A murmur of consensus rose from the group.

James stroked his chin and looked down as if studying cracks in the sidewalk. "All right. Thanks." He trudged on, an emptiness burrowing inside him. Dark thoughts raced through his mind. Maybe something happened to him. Maybe he been jumped by thugs and laying in a hospital somewhere. James went to bed for the rest of the day.

The following day, with a hollowness burgeoning, he struggled up and went to Mount of Olives Baptist Church to seek solace. He tried to concentrate on the sermon, but his mind kept returning to Mitchell, and he left the service as bereft as ever. Every morning after work he trod the blocks from the studio in concentric squares searching for Mitchell, asking folks if they had seen anyone fitting his description. Each afternoon he returned home in despair. He decided he'd give it seven days.

James sank into despair, like he was wrapped in thick cotton batting for protection from the world around him. At the same time the city retreated under a blanket of gray skies, occasionally releasing layers of ice and snow. He often skipped going to the carriage house after work and curled inside his bed to sleep or read scripture.

His spirits began to stir in the new year when warmer days brought an early thaw, but forever his eyes swept the faces of young men rushing past him on the street, hoping for a glimmer of recognition.

He returned to his mission with renewed dedication, speaking aloud as if Mitchell was still by his side while he worked. With divine guidance the Assembly grew. Year piled upon year, and the project flowered into a roomful of creations that shone like sunlight. A bulletin board on the back wall displayed a copied verse from Proverbs: "Where there is no vision, the people perish."

God sent an angel to oversee the project. James folded to his knees and prayed aloud. "Revelation. Separation. Holy Nation." He commanded James to record on twelve sacred tablets the words He would dictate. The tablets were to hang on the walls of the Assembly. Only 'The Chosen' in the End of Days would receive the gift of understanding to decipher the meaning of the symbols and coded language written on the tablets.

Over the years, he occasionally attended local churches, harboring hope he would meet a holy woman to help him, but that never panned out. The preachers aggravated him with their rules. Feeling lonely, once he invited two acquaintances to come after church to see something important he was working on. When they stepped inside the carriage house, James swept his arm in welcome and said, "This is my life's work. Before I die, it will be finished." The two men stood mouths agape, one with arms crossed high on his chest until he walked over to one of the tablets on the wall. Sticking his nose inches from it he squinted, scrunching up his face in confusion. "James, what kind of writing is this here? I can't read it."

When James said that he wasn't allowed to tell anyone, the man raised his eyebrows at the other visitor and said, "You don't say." Then the two of them stood around hemming and hawing in that awkward way people do when they don't know what to say. As soon as he could, James ushered them out, relieved to see the back of them.

Piled neatly on a table, eight composition books were crammed with thoughts he wrote down over the years. One was entitled "St. James: The Book of the 7 Dispensation." Every day he wrote in his room toward dusk before he went to work. Brimming with Bible references, verses, and symbols, he had devised a code so if someone found the notebooks, he wouldn't understand what was written. At the bottom of every page was the word "Revelation."

Finally, the time has come for the Throne of Heaven to be finished. Leaning over, James removes the final burned out light bulb from the burlap sack. Wrapped in the day's newspaper, he carefully unrolls it, cradling it in his hand. He grows pensive. Holding the bulb close to his face, he studies the delicate filament looped inside and imagines. One man come up with the idea of this little thing and now we can light up the dark. Maybe a angel come to Mr. Thomas Edison too.

Pulling out balls of misshapen aluminum foil, he sets them on his lap. Expertly wrapping the last bulb, borne of countless repetition, he leaves a skirt for attaching it with tacks at the bottom. Pressing and plying he adds another layer and a third. In his hands, the material transforms from pocked foil into hammered silver. Rolling, molding, folding, the orb soon glows on the altar.

The pain comes in waves now. Clutching his stomach, James breathes in shallow puffs to ease the pressure. He teeters up a step ladder and steadies himself. With trembling fingers, he attaches two words in silver foil to a space above the royal Throne, then raises his arms toward heaven. "Hallelujah! Praise God!" Bold, imperfect letters appear suspended: "Fear Not."

Over a 14-year period James Hampton created 180 objects of visionary religious folk art, considered the greatest of its kind in existence. It is now part of the permanent collection of the Smithsonian American Folk Art exhibition in Washington, D.C.

Piano Lessons

"Guess what happened at the racetrack today." Mom barely waited for me to slide onto the passenger seat after picking me up from middle school. I hadn't seen her so giddy since before Dad moved out.

"You won't believe it. I won the daily double!" Glancing at me beneath gray curls, blue eyes sparkling behind half-bifocal glasses.

"No way!" I squealed. Bouncing up and down, I shoved unruly tendrils of auburn hair behind my ears in a nervous habit.

Mom worked at Montgomery Ward in the fabric department. On her day off, she stuffed her plump body into a polyester pantsuit, and when harness races were on, went with a friend to Laurel Raceway. I giggled when she first told me, imagining how out of place she must look there. Twice she had taken me with her, and I saw people of every size and description, so I wasn't embarrassed to be with her.

The day after she chose the winners in a daily double, a truncated, upright piano stood in our living room when I got home from school. Mom spent all her winnings on it so I could resume piano lessons. They had ceased in second grade, when my teacher discovered I had poor eyesight. Money designated for learning piano was shifted to buy glasses instead.

The following week Mom investigated leads from coworkers and friends to find a piano instructor willing to accept a fourteen-year-old student. Mrs. Williams lived half an hour away, and agreed to teach me. The following Thursday, Mom drove me to her house for my first lesson.

After introductions, Mrs. Williams handed me John Thompson's First Grade Book. Pressing it open to the first page, we read instructions aloud. "Middle C is home for your hands." She demonstrated a soft curve of fingers on keys. Soon, my fingers crawled up and down scales. Subsequent lessons covered quarter, half and whole notes, each session teaching what to me was a secret language.

At first, I practiced every day. I loved the set goals each week and how repetition elicited praise from Mrs. Williams. I progressed to songs with flats and sharps, learned when to rest or play andante.

The next school year I completed the Second Grade Book. Mom insisted on a solo concert. Each composition was followed by her enthusiastic applause. I giggled and said, "I made mistakes in that last one."

She laughed too. "That doesn't matter a bit, honey. Look what you can play. It's wonderful!"

I was a sophomore when Mrs. Williams placed the Third Grade Book on the music stand, I thumbed through to see the difficulty. Complicated adaptations filled multiple pages. I shoved my hair behind my ears and chewed on my lower lip. Sensing my nervousness, she said, "Don't be discouraged. You'll take it one step at a time. We begin with an American folk song. I know you like those."

That fall, Dad called to invite me to a National Symphony Orchestra concert at Constitution Hall in Washington, D.C. I'd never heard a live orchestra. Butterflies tickled my insides as we walked into the hall. I was glad Mom said I should dress up, because everyone wore fancy clothes. A man in a suit handed us a program, and another helped us find assigned seats. The performer in a tuxedo played a grand piano. It was magic! Music fell over me like a waterfall. A flurry of emotions rushed through me. During intermission, I said to Dad, "I wish I could play like that." He smiled and said, "He's been doing this for years, but even he had to take lessons."

I progressed, but practice now bit into my free time with friends in the neighborhood. The effort was worth it when I conquered Hungarian Rhapsody No. 2. Mrs. Williams put a gold star beside the title. To celebrate completion of Book Three, Mom and I jumped in the old Rambler and headed to Chandler's Drug Store soda fountain for a Coke float.

When I turned sixteen, Mom allowed me to double date. Naturally, boys, social life, and homework absorbed my attention. Piano practice slipped down on my priority list. Scores were more difficult in Book Four, yet I practiced minimally. At lessons, Mrs. Williams often tapped the end of her pencil over a measure. "Again. You can do better."

Practice became a chore. One night over dinner, I mentioned I'd like to stop my lessons for a while. Mom flattened her lips into a stern line. "A skill worth learning isn't easy. If it was, everyone could do it. That doesn't mean you give up. Remember how hard you practiced before the recital last year? Everyone complimented you. I want you to keep going."

I persevered. With more practice, my technique improved. I tackled Tchaikovsky's *Pathetique,* almost throwing my hands up in frustration. An innate stubbornness kicked in. I practiced daily, and it began to flow. With it, came a surprising increase in self-confidence.

Mom's work hours changed. A new boss scheduled her two nights a week. I started babysitting, and spent more time with my boyfriend. Practice ceased except for sheet music I chose to play. By this time, I was driving myself to lessons, and began making excuses for not going.

As I pushed boundaries of independence, Mom and I engaged in heated discussions. One night we settled on the sofa for the Nightly News, as was our habit. Having stood on her feet for the eight-hour shift, Mom sighed and lifted tired legs onto the coffee table.

I said, "My term paper is due in two weeks. I'm feeling overwhelmed with homework. Final exams are coming up, and

I've barely had time to study. Could I take a break from piano lessons? Summer is only weeks away."

A rueful look crossed her face. "Once you stop, it's hard to go back. I know you don't think so, but believe me."

"I can play most music I pick up." Running to the piano bench, I snatched sheet music I'd bought the week before with money from babysitting. "See? I'll still practice some; I promise." Besides, you'll have the money for something else instead of lessons."

Usually, she cajoled or made me feel guilty when she wanted me to do something against my will. This time she shook her head. "Don't use that as an excuse. I want you to continue, but I can't make you. I know someday you'll regret it." She stood and shuffled to the kitchen, poured herself a cup of tea. Frowning, she returned to the sofa. "You have to call Mrs. Williams and tell her yourself that you're quitting. She's invested a lot of time teaching you."

I called her the next day. She said she was sorry to hear it. "You've made wonderful progress. I've enjoyed teaching you." I thanked her and clung to the invitation she offered to return in the summer.

For the remainder of the school year, I played sporadically. I didn't resume lessons that summer. When I did play, it wasn't from Thompson's, but sheet music of movie scores. My favorite was "Lara's Theme" from *Dr. Zhivago*, however, I never achieved the fluidity I yearned for.

Sometimes Mom and I reminisced about days when the family was together. At her urging, I'd pull out a tattered hymnal and play her requests. We'd sing aloud.

After high school, I attended ITT Business Institute in Washington and moved to an apartment in the city. A demanding career rarely allowed an opportunity to pursue hobbies. Occasionally, slivers of time offered the chance for my fingers to recall what I knew was disintegrating. When I thought about Mom's sacrifice, not just of money but taking me to and from lessons, my favorite scores soothed my soul and my conscience. I'd tell myself, this time I'll practice every day, even if it's fifteen minutes. I'll get it back.

Marriage and babies of my own precipitated more moves. The piano and music, including Thompson's books, carefully packed in a box, I brought with me. Time and neglect rusted my ability. The last effort I made to play, I had forgotten some meanings of music's language, like meeting a friend after a long absence and you're both at a loss for words.

Mom passed away.

Down the stairway of years, I finally surrendered and sold the piano. Unconsciously, hope hibernated within me because I kept the books and sheet music.

In the spring of 2020, under stay-at-home restrictions due to Covid-19, the world grew quiet. Sounds I'd never heard before accompanied me through muted days, church bells in the village, wind soughing through the neighbor's willow tree. One morning, a symphony of birdsong surprised me with its clarity. Thoughts turned to other music, and how Mom had given me something precious which I had squandered, lost. Days stretched before me like blank pages until I heard the birds singing.

With the pandemic stimulus check, I bought a used piano from a friend who was downsizing. The day it was delivered, I sanitized every inch. Using a shammy cloth, I polished it in small circles, my hands learning the scars and imperfections in the piano's warm, walnut case. I bathed each ivory key, ebony flat and sharp. Only then did I allow my fingers to press and hear every note. Dulcet tones came alive, still in tune after the move. Settling into position on the bench I reached for Thompson's First Grade Book, and turned to Lesson One.

Dreams in Deep Water

At the end of the dock, Naia's moon-colored arms stretched out and up above her head. Rising on her toes, she propelled her lissome, arched body toward the lake's surface. It cracked like a fragile egg. Below, feathery flora caressed her body. Anticipation of being swallowed by water was as sensuous as a tongue on her skin. She longed for its touch.

She planned to explore one of the caves tucked discreetly half a mile south of the cottage. Locals referred to summer homes as camps. Finding her freestyle, rhythmic strokes, the lake flooded her with a primal feeling. It was as if the water retained some ancient power from the Ice Age when it was formed by a receding glacier. Each time she swam, the sense grew stronger until she was convinced there was something magical about it.

Lifting her head, she scanned the shore for the cave entrance and found the low-hanging willow that obscured the opening. Entering the mouth of the cave, she gained purchase on a flat boulder created by storms pushing water in and out of the pocket cavity. A tangle of sunlight through willow fronds lit the cave. Tufts of lichen clung to the ceiling. A gentle wake slapping against stone reminded her of a heartbeat.

Her fingers explored a high, rock shelf and touched a nest-like indentation formed over millennia. At the far side, her hand nudged a stone the shape of an egg. As she brought it into the filtered light, she pondered whether it could actually be a fossilized egg of an ancient bird. For safekeeping, she placed it in her swimsuit between her breasts.

Searching for fossils or unusual rocks had been a hobby since childhood. Naia was enchanted by the idea of holding remains of creatures that lived millions of years ago. A collection from Crystal Lake was growing on the porch of the cottage, as a reminder of this place when she was stranded in front of her seventh-grade class. Here, at the edge of sunlight, life in the city with Alex seemed as far away as her own junior high. She took a deep breath and swam out of the cave, luxuriating in the moments underwater, until the need for air forced her to surface.

The previous winter, Naia had stumbled upon an ad in the *New York Times* Weekend section offering a cottage rental on Crystal Lake, "*the second cleanest lake in the country.*" It was only four hours from their apartment on the lower east side. Though brutal wind and snow often raged outside in winter, her memory catapulted her to the oppressive heat of summers spent in the non-air-conditioned apartment she fled every afternoon. If she complained to Alex, he retorted, "Need I remind you, this apartment was a gift from my father so it's free except for amenity fees. When we moved here, we *both* knew there would be sacrifices living in an old building. Things are quirky and don't work like they do in a glass tower. Remember, you said you didn't care as long as it was in a good location and had character."

Naia had secured the cabin for six weeks beginning the third weekend of June.

Days in the classroom crammed with restless and unruly thirteen-year-olds were softened by anticipation of weeks by a lake in the woods. An image filled her mind with birdsong, frogs, and lapping water instead of traffic, shouts, and noise of the city. Alex would fly to Syracuse on weekends, and they would invite friends to stay too.

It had sounded idyllic. Days unfurled like sails, blank and pure, waiting for her to fill them. For the first few weeks, it was perfect. In the middle of the third week, things began to change. Alex called to say he had an emergency at work. He was an architect with a growing reputation. Problems had arisen with the design. It's always like this near the end of a project, as you know," he moaned.

"Oh, I'm so sorry you can't come." Naia couldn't keep the disappointment from leaching through the phone. "I miss you, but I understand. "Work emergencies" had been a recurring excuse for not joining her on the previous vacation at the Cape. The following Thursday, he called to say he had come down with a summer cold and didn't have the strength to travel.

"The Myers are coming up. It's been planned for months. And it's the weekend of the Classic Boat Show. Just take cold meds. You can rest once you get here." She pleaded, "Alex, I need you. Sam and Renee are expecting you to be here, especially Sam."

He was not persuaded. Naia sensed something amiss but felt powerless to do anything about it from 200 miles away. Submerging her suspicions, she immersed herself in the beauty of the cabin and its natural setting. Still, a prescient shadow lingered over her.

The weekend with Sam and Renee was not what she had hoped, however, they managed to have a delightful time. The highlight was walking in the quaint village at the head of the lake, with its artisans' arts and crafts plus antique shops. Sam found the classic wooden boats at the show fascinating.

"They are pretty when you see the workmanship up close," Naia said. "The thing I don't like is their engines are really loud. I wish they would outlaw them on the lake. You'll see what I mean when the contestants have the ride-by boat parade I've read about."

Sam patted her on the shoulder, "Of course, you have a right to an opinion. It just means no one here gives a damn what it is." The three of them burst into laughter.

Naia said, "Come on, you two. Let's go back to the camp and go swimming. On the way, I'll stop by the local farmer's roadside vegetable stand and buy something for dinner.

You won't believe how fresh and delicious it is, and cheap!"

Alex flew up the following Friday as scheduled. At the airport, Naia waited at curbside to greet him. When she spotted his dark hair above most travelers she smiled and waved.

As he approached the car, she noticed his briefcase, which he tossed on the back seat. He gave her an air kiss and fastened his seatbelt. Her heart sank. After two weeks apart, he had brought work with him.

On the way to camp, he filled her in on details of what had transpired at the office. She listened politely and finally interrupted him. "Alex, can't you forget about work for the next 48 hours. It will be gone before you know it, so let's make the most of every minute." She was determined to make the weekend as perfect as possible.

"Of course, you're right. I do need to de-stress."

"How about a swim before dinner?" Naia asked.

"Good idea."

Naia felt Alex seemed to have erected a barrier between them. Perhaps it was all in her mind, simply the imagination of a jealous wife thinking other women were after her handsome, successful husband. There's probably nothing to worry about, she tried to convince herself.

After a brief swim, they faced the challenging steps to the cottage. She quickly changed into dry clothes. "Would you like a drink before dinner?" She had bought a six-pack of Stella Artois, his favorite.

"I'd love a scotch," Alex said and strolled from the bedroom wearing khaki shorts and a deep blue polo shirt the color of his eyes.

Nonplussed, Naia plucked a glass from atop a small table she used for liquor. "Coming right up." After pouring three fingers' of Glenfiddich, she handed it to him as he walked onto the porch.

Sitting in a Adirondack chair, he took a sip. "Aaah. Perfect."

She poured herself a glass of pinot Grigio and slid into a

Bentwood rocker beside him. A short while later, drowsy from alcohol, he dozed off, his head lolling on one shoulder. Naia read a chapter of a novel borrowed from the local library. Soon, she fell asleep too. Upon waking, the lake called to her. I think I'm becoming addicted, she thought. I can hardly really resist. An uneasiness lingered until Alex awoke so she could prepare dinner. She handed him a bag of corn. "How about shucking the corn and I'll fire up the grill for two promising tenderloins?"

Over dinner on the screened porch, they chatted about what she'd done the previous weeks. She enthused about her adventures, especially finding the "egg." Plucking it from the fossil collection, she placed it in his hand. "It does look like an egg, but I'm not sure it is. It's awfully heavy."

"I refuse to be dissuaded by a skeptic. Only positive energy is allowed in." He shrugged and raised his arms in surrender. She asked how he had spent his free time, but his answers were suspiciously vague.

"I have to tell you, that dinner was amazing. I don't think I can move." Naia walked outside. "Come see the stars." She pointed out the constellations. "It's so beautiful. I even saw a falling star this week."

They made love that night, but Naia didn't feel the spark that used to surge through her body. It almost seemed perfunctory on his end and left her feeling empty. She lay awake, wondering if it was her or Alex.

Early Saturday morning, Alex filled a thermos with water and said, "I think I'll take the kayak out while the lake is calm." He didn't ask her to go, but she preferred to swim anyway. They descended to the pebbled beach and stopped alongside two overturned lime-green, molded plastic kayaks.

"Life vests are in the shed there," Naia said, her head tilting to a weathered building on the left. An aluminum shed nestled against the steep hill at its back.

Alex found the door was stuck. He shoved it with his shoulder, then yanked it, muttering obscenities. It gave way and out tumbled an assortment of lakeside equipment: life vests, double-ended paddles, and skis. He leaned over and picked through the vests until he found one big enough for his six-foot-two-inch frame.

From a short distance, she watched. It obscured to her that when he was absent, she forgot about his flaws, the impatience with anything the least bit difficult. After twelve years of marriage, she had learned to ignore it. Somewhere on the internet, she had read that this action signaled a latent hostility.

~~~~~~~~~~~~~~~~~~

She ordered herself to gain control. At the kitchen table she slid a nearby notepad to start a list of everything she had to do. She remembered that her prescription for Prozac had run out the week before, and she needed it more than ever now. That went first on the list. Her mind was muddled. I need time to think about all of this. She went into the bedroom and got dressed, then headed to the pharmacy.

After a quick stop at a local deli, she drove back to camp. Home again, the temperature was perfect, so she headed to the lake. In the water, thoughts of Alex and her uncertain future were replaced with concentration on her surroundings. The moment she stood on land, her worries insinuated themselves into her mind again. I have three weeks to figure out what I'm going to do.

Inside the camp she headed straight to the fridge. She was famished. It was hard to function without protein for fuel, and all she'd had was a bagel for breakfast. She pried a strawberry yogurt from a six-pack, and spooned it down without sitting. Craving something sweet, she riffled a drawer where a cache of energy bars was stashed, and chose one with chocolate.

Looking to the notepad, next was "Pick up camp, sweep kitchen and porch." She tuned the radio to a local oldies station, and attacked the dirt and dishes, while melodies from younger years raised her mood.

The rising heat created pearls on her forehead that leaked into her eyes. She need to cool down and the lake beckoned her again, like a Greek siren. She couldn't resist. Having learned it was dangerous to swim beyond the outer edge of docks extending into the lake at every camp, she wore a bright swim cap, and kept an eye out for motorized crafts. The water soothed her psyche and she kept going until she reached beyond the point of visibility from her own camp. It was the furthest she had ventured and the longest she had swum. The freestyle stroke was like freedom, lending her the sense that she could swim forever, but her inner safety alarm insisted she turn around. The shore of her camp at last came into view, relieving anxiety.

By the time she reached the dock she was pleasantly tired. Diving deep one more time, she swam underwater until she ran out of breath. Breaking the surface with a toss of her head, she looked at her watch, and congratulated herself on a new personal best, having stayed underwater over a minute. Despite the tiredness, she loved how her body tingled, every cell alive.

On the lounger, she leaned over to dry her legs, and noticed an iridescent coating on them. She wondered if she had swum through an oil slick from a leaking boat and tried rubbing it, but it wouldn't come off. She surmised it was a trick of the light.

The following predawn, her world shrouded in fog, she made a bold decision. A modest person all her life, she had never been skinny dipping, though friends in high school had tried to coax her to join them. Shedding her pajamas and underwear, she said sarcastically, "The saying goes 'Today is the first day of the rest of my life.' So, I'll begin it like I did my birth: in the nude!"

Glancing at her torso, she gasped. A pink rash stippled her stomach like Himalayan salt. It didn't itch, but she surmised she must be allergic to something in the lake. All was silent around her in the predawn. Munching on a cinnamon bun she had bought when she was in the village the day before.

Weak sunlight crawled over the hill. Dark clouds shrouded

the lake. A rumble of thunder echoed through the hollows and a sweet smell of rain permeated the air. Moments later, a slash of lightning ripped the clouds. From the porch, she watched the rain march down the lake in a perfect line, like soldiers in formation. It quickly filled a nearby gully, splashing over boulders, in its rush to the lake. Lightning played a prelude to thunder's brash cymbal on places around her. The rain was so thick the lake was barely visible.

She sighed. "Foiled again."

Slipping on her pajamas again, she made herbal tea. With a fragrant mugful, she strolled onto the porch to listen to the storm. The temperature was plummeting, and she snuggled under an ecru and blue throw. Strain of her limbo state had drained her energy reserve. After several minutes, she fell into a light sleep.

Seconds after waking, the net of knowledge trapped her again. She tried to block the overwhelming problems she faced. The storm had passed, leaving behind slow drips from firs and hemlocks. Pulling up her pajama top, she checked the rash. She rushed to the bedroom and snatched the lotion from the dresser and spread it liberally until her skin was slick.

Taking the novel from the bedside table, she flopped in the rocker to read. The mystery was finally solved. For a time, she wallowed in the mire of an uncertain future.

Later, light from a full moon streamed through the porch screens lending a golden cast to the plank floors. It was bright enough that she could see the steps to the lake. "I'm going in!"

Descending to the shore, a delicious calm enveloped her. Waves quietly licked the beach. She let them roll over her feet and discovered it was warmer than the air. She undressed, folded her clothes, and placed them on the lounge chair. The chilly air rippled her skin into goose bumps. Beneath a cloudless sky, stars shown above. Boldly, she walked to the end of the pier and dove in.

Minutes passed. Naia began breathing underwater. A cascade

of pain ripped through her body as if her internal organs were contracting. She wondered if she was dying. This finally dissipated so that she noticed a school of trout maneuver their pectoral fins while moving to encircle her. A larger fish, obviously the leader, sniffed her, then emitted a mysterious sound. She converged with the school. Mimicking the fishes' movements, Naia gathered her strength, and with a powerful swish of her caudal fin, disappeared into the deep.

Judy McGinn discovered her love of stories at a very young age, as she was the progeny of southern storytellers. Her fiction was first printed in Cork, Ireland, where she won first place in prose in *The Cork Literary Review Writing Contest*. Her short stories appeared twice in *The South Carolina Review*. She won first prize in prose for *The Vinnie Ream Short Story Contest* sponsored by the National League of American Pen Women. Her stories have been shortlisted in *The Fish Short Story Contest*, and long listed in *William Faulkner/Wisdom Short Story Contest*. Her poetry and prose have appeared in many anthologies such as *Lun'Allure*, commemorating the 50th anniversary of the original moon landing, and *Earth Care*, a collection about the global warming crisis (Willett Press in 2022).

Printed in the USA
CPSIA information can be obtained
at www.ICGtesting.com
JSHW030021210823
46912JS00012B/147

9 781957 221113